Charlotte and the Chickenman

Charlotte and the Chickenman

Aina Hunter

WHISK(E)Y TIT
VT & NTC

Published in the United States by Whisk(e)y Tit: www.whiskeytit.com. If you wish to use or reproduce all or part of this book for any means, please let the author and publisher know. You're pretty much required to, legally.

ISBN 978-1-952600-40-1

Cover art by Marjorie Ann Williams.

Edited by Meagan Masterman.

Contents

Prologue

"Cell meat makes great bacon. Also the ham, the smoked turkey. It's good for sandwiches," P'tit Luc bends his wrist in a precise gesture, then draws his spoon across the surface of his bowl of consommé towards his mouth.

"Hold that thought," Margot lifts one manicured finger. "The first taste must be savored!"

"This is true," says P'tit Luc genially. Gestured in my direction. "I am prepared to wager twenty—non—fifty dollars! That is how certain I am that you have never before tasted consommé this delicious."

"So fragrant," I agreed, willing myself not to spill.

"And each course to follow will be like this," says Fradine, "they never disappoint!" Turning to her wife she add, "But you know, I think I have discovered the secret. They must use a sort of gumbo *file* – just taste it again! "

Spoon in mid-air, Big Luc closed her eyes to consider. Then, beaming at her wife said, "Sassafras! Genius, my dear."

Margot said, "Madame Fradine has a very fine palate. In the States you say, *quesque on dit*, supertaster!"

I wasn't sure but nodded anyway.

"And also hamburgers, hotdogs, anything ground-up," p't Luc was back on the original topic. "But it cannot take the place of a drumstick until they figure out the bone!"

Margot said, "It isn't healthy. It's just as much cholesterol as common bone meat."

"I am not debating the health of it," he returns. "But we cannot deny that Haitian people, we like to suck the bone! I am *unsatisfied* if I cannot suck the marrow!"

Fradine says, reminiscently, "*Mon P'tit* has always loved the drumstick."

"And the wishbone!"

Big Luc said, "Yes, the wishbone. You should have seen these two, placing bets—"

"Those were the good days. We could raise chickens then."

"Not to sell, you understand," said Fradine, addressing me. "But just for the family it was okay. Every Sunday I'd slow-roast a fresh, whole chicken. Mon P'tit Luc would be so excited to break the wishbone with his *grandpere*."

"Grandfather?" I asked, antenna up.

"We used to call Big Luc Grand Luc, you see. And then p'tit Luc began to say Grandpere, and it stuck."

"Sadly enough," said Big Luc, "My most vivid memories are quite disturbing. I was expected, once a week, to commit a terrible act of betrayal. I called it Bloody Saturday, because every bloody Saturday I had to kill and pluck a poor chicken—with no help from these people!"

P'tit Luc gulped his wine, chortling. Fradine and Margot struggled not to laugh.

Big Luc made a wide gesture over her family, "These bone meat lovers here never once offered to help. In fact, most Saturday afternoons they were nowhere to be found!"

A giggle escaped..

"Why do you laugh?" Big Luc demanded, puffed up with mock outrage. "It was not fair!"

"No, it was not fair. That part was not fair," said Fradine; both of us laughing by then.

"Those who want bone-meat should be required to

participate in the entire process," this from Margot, strategically inserting herself at the half-way point between both of her mother-in-laws to be.

P'tit Luc, accepting more bread from a server, changed the subject. "Many people are still eating bone-meat in the States, *pas non*?"

"Yeah but mostly in the conflict regions down south and the semi-autonomous states," I said.

"And is it not true that you pay more for the breast, for the white meat?"

"Well I don't, not for years I haven't, but yes, people pay more for the breast."

Margot raised one carefully arched brow and said, "But dark meat has more flavor! It's more. . . qu'est qu'on dit . . . wet?"

"Juicy," I agreed.

"Have you ever wondered," P'tit Luc said reflectively, "why dark meat is dark? I mean, why is it dark?

Margot said, "One could just as easily ask, why is the white meat white—see how that works?"

P'tit Luc, annoyed, switched to rapid Kreyol. "*Comprenez? Pourquoi-ça ? Some meat, c'est brun at les autres sont blanc. It can be on the same animal, pas non?"*

Margot said, "Yes, my dear, but it is in how you phrase the question. Those less charitable than we assembled here might see evidence of latent Eurin-colonial bias."

Fradine said, "Your fiancée is right, Mon P'tit. Instead of asking the white thing why it is white, you ask the dark thing, 'why are you dark?'"

"Dark meat is more vascular,"says Big Luc, with authority. "The tissue is dark because it is full of blood vessels and capillaries. The legs, the wing, the back—they need constant blood flow to do all the work."

P'tit Luc hooted. "That sounds familiar! The white part just sits there, existing just to be carried around!"

I could feel Margot's side eye heating up my cheek and my fingers felt cold. I looked to Fradine in time to see her lip twitch. Both Lucs reached for their napkins—simultaneously, eyes averted. Hunching over my bowl, I muttered, "a god-damned shame is whatitis." It was the voice of a dank, bitter, bone-tired American black woman. I'm really not a reliably funny person, but when I'm funny I'm pretty good. The table exploded in laughter. Fradine reached over to fist bump. Margot lifted her glass of beaujolais, her smile broad and genuine.

We didn't really straighten up until each of our five servers had assembled once again, in erect, tuxedoed dignity, one behind each of our chairs. Spiced, stuffed sea vegetable in a fragile tempura was next. My stomach growled; I was suddenly very hungry. Hungrier than I'd been in weeks, it seemed.

The mood at the table turned refective when Margot mused, "They say faux-human cell meat tastes like pork. I've never had pork. I can't imagine it."

"Think of cell beef only more tender," says P'tit Luc.

"I can think of quite a few folks I wouldn't mind digesting," I said.

"Bien sûr, but surely we speak of Epicurean cannibalism? This is distinct from the headhunter. Or the survivor of a natural disaster driven to cannibalism by desperation. Who kills out of necessity." This from Luc, pushing back his eye glasses.

"The serial killer?"

Luc was in full anthropologist mode, now, and the rest of us settled back and got comfortable. "The earliest references to what we now call 'epicurean cannibalism'" are found in ancient Chinese cookbooks," she began. "Some of the most interesting research was done back in the 1980's by Professor Key Ray Chong. Again, we are speaking of a brand of cannibalism that is culturally sanctioned. Not desperate people avoiding starvation—that is commonplace throughout history. But epicurean cannibalism, here we speak of something special."

"You never hear about it, though," I said.

"The Judeo-Christian world has an almost pathological aversion to cannibalism. We can trace this fear and loathing to the Old Testament. In much of the Americas, Africa and Asia, however...the relative absence of dietary restrictions in, for example, the Confucian tradition made it an easier sell—"

"What about Buddhism?" I asked. "Ahimsa—do no harm to other sentients?"

Margot said, "Are you a Buddhist?"

"Not really. Aspiring, I guess. I'm not even a perfect vegan," I was thinking about the spider.

Fradine sighed. "There may come a time to kill, at least that's what the Obos say."

Big Luc said, "Chong compiled hundreds of recipes for human meat, with separate sections for smoked, broiled, baked, sun-dried even! Mostly from the Tsui dynasty.

I wondered aloud how they decided who was to be eaten.

"Your very reasonable question has many complex, human-sized answers. Love and hate. Filial piety and Punishment. Perceived Nutritional or medical benefits. Availability and abundance."

"Perceived deliciousness!" This from P'tit Luc, before making a show of burying his face in his fiancées bosom. Margot yelped.

Espresso and cake came and went. And then the ferry home. I just chewed and listened. Kept chewing and chewing although there was nothing left in my mouth.

Charlotte and the Chickenman

1.

White Meat

Charlotte takes communion

Anchored off the south-eastern coast of Haiti is a grand old ship. A refurbished galleon. Built in Liverpool in the late 1700s, she was born cursed —a slaver. For decades the slow ship hissed and groaned, hull packed with the stench of human-animal misery. But not anymore! Today the refurbished Mahogany Queen is home to an exclusive supper club featuring Kreyol-French fine dining and live jazz! It is not terribly unusual for a famous artist from Cuba, Kingston or New York to drop in via Airtaxi. They come from as far away as Australia, Capetown. Even Seoul! Who knows? There is no way of knowing how far word has spread by now. Next year will mark her 25th anniversary . . .

How to describe! I will first tell you that the interior is a vision of reclaimed copper and sea glass and bone —all embedded in tropical hardwood. But to see the true miracle, one must look very close. And when you do, here comes the surprise! Gentle faces grow visible and they appear to regard you right back! It is trompe l'oeil, you are understanding this? Blue black copper brown faces—they are coming through the wall—the innermost hull on both sides—konprann?

Yes, this is true! Se vre! These phenotypes were conceived—are still being conceived—from DNA recovered from the original wood. The lead sculptress is also a geneticist—you've heard of her work, ouais?

I shook my head no.

Pity, she said, patting my knee.

Anyway, the dining room is truly extraordinary. The deck itself is glass wood, beams and plates, so the hull is flooded in diffused light. Attached is a floating greenhouse for sea vegetables prepared to compliment the most superior cuts of bone meat—oh dear. For a moment I forgot —not to worry, we are not big meat eaters. That is just a stereotype and we would never pressure you to eat anything that disagrees with you in any way! You will see!

Charlotte, Charlotte. You might be the luckiest unlucky woman in Haiti, do you know that? It seems that my sweet panda, our Big Luc, has taken a scholarly interest in your cultural development. Therefore, before you fly back, she means to treat the whole family to an evening on the Mahogany, provided our reservation is accepted. Last minute strings have already been pulled.

Me: Really?

Fradine: It is true! It's well worth the expense because it has been too long since we've had a nice evening out, and in truth, we've been meaning to treat p'tit Luc and Margot before the wedding. You know, my dear, we were surprised and saddened when you left the table like that. I do not like to think that you feel so alone in this world. It is unnecessary!

Anyway, where were we? The atmosphere on board is pure luxury, no detail left uncurated. Only the finest Haitian cotton for table linens, chairs and booths upholstered in the buttery leather of the greater Antilles. The silver is real, the prices extortionate. The menu is prix-fixe and the protocol old-fashioned. You might find it a little stuffy. Bien. This is to be expected as the governing membership of the Mahogany Queen is quite elderly.

Me: The Old Black Ones?
Fradine: Ouais, ouais. The Old Black Ones. So you do know a little history!
Me: I'm really not that young, you know.
Fradine: You are still just a little thing. In your head, but that's okay, Chou-Chou.

Anyway. Today the Mahogany Queen is leading her

third life—her best, most gracious life! That is what Nicole Thibodeaux likes to say, you know? Which reminds me, the Gracious Living finale airs first thing tomorrow! You are welcome to join me for guided conscious movement in the watch room, but know that I am strict with my routine. Yes?

I nodded through the dark.

I think you should try. Why not join us—just myself and Luc—for breakfast first. Have a little coffee, you don't have to eat.

I was still nodding.

Perhaps you will, perhaps you will not. I cannot tell.

Anyway, where were we? <u>*La Reign Acajou*</u>, the Mahogany Queen. Although destined for noble purpose, the Mahogany was born a wretched slaver and she did slave. For decades she slaved, back and forth across the Atlantic. She would not be free until Henri Caesar and his brothers made them redundant—you understand? I am speaking now of the Eurindigenous captain and crew, *konprann*?

I nodded.

So you see, in this way she was reborn a pirate! The second ship under the command of captain Henri Caesar. But this much you must already know, yes? Everyone knows this story, I think.

Me: Not in detail. I like to hear you tell it. He wasn't really a cannibal, was he?

Fradine: Oh dear. I fear your head is filled with Eurin-colonial nonsense.

Of course they called him a cannibal, but this is just racism. Fear begets fear, you know. So many bad names for poor Henri Caesar! They call him a ghoul, a coward, a gangster and, worse, they call him a wish. *Konpronne sa*?

I nodded.

I will give you the truth: He never knew his mother, most likely she was his father's slave. His father, a connoisseur and a collector, raised him with that peculiar privilege then-afforded certain *enfant milat*. Mulâtre. *Konprann* "milat?"

Yeah, I could guess but I shook my head no anyway. Fradine reached out to flip my lower lip with her finger, the way you do pouting children.

We both laughed and she said, "It's a privilege without agency, *ma pauvre*. Anyway. Where were we? Little Henri. He was certainly his father's son; they looked so much alike! The boy developed a refined palate and a passion for discourse and wine pairing. Most evenings, after dinner, Henri would read aloud to his father who was something of a . . . how do you say . . .Orientalist? *Ouais, d'accord.* Yes, so together they read French translations of

Chinese texts. Among his favorite tales was the story of a notorious flesh-eating general of the Sui Dynasty who ate the flesh of his enemies! Henri loved these stories and treasured this time with his father.

Monsieur Arnaut loved his son, but from all reports, the gentleman was a coward. And Henri was growing big and tall —and far too inquisitive—to pass as a houseboy. There was quite a bit of pressure from all sides. Arnaut's new wife was unhappy with the situation, and Arnaut never registered the boy with the colonial authorities, never officially gave his son his last name. No last name, no legitimacy. Henri was first confused and then enraged; Arnaut, of course, was racked with guilt. It got so that Arnaut was ashamed to face his son and refused, for months, to even see him. He locked himself up in his bedrooms for weeks. And then, on the eve of Henri's sixteenth birthday, Arnaut arranged for him to be kidnapped from his bed, stuffed into a burlap sack and carried miles away to work at the sawmill.

Day in, day out. Splitting rock-hard mahogany logs into boards in the choking heat was punishing labor alone. But it was the demon overseer the other men called "Dinclinson" who made life for the discarded teenager worse. Dinclinson, you see, was notorious in that part of the country. He used rape and psychological torture to keep 'his boys' under control and reveled in the fear and loathing he inspired. He told Henri and the other young men that he was possessed by the intranquil spirit of the same name and that if they betrayed him he would follow them to hell. Whatever his motivations, Dinclinson would cruelly use the sensitive young man for many years to follow. He would one day regret this. Revolution was in the air, once again. Some say it blew in from Paris when the guillotine dropped. It was 1790 when the shrieking winds swept through the cane fields. Henri La Scie was ready. La Scie is saw — konpronne? The saw? Not to look-see, to cut." Fradine flattened her hand, jerked it forward and back. I nodded.

"With a lethal pair of knives he'd fashioned from a two-man saw, Henri La Scie butchered the overseer and then fled into the hills with a gang of marrons."

"Maroons? I've heard of the-"

"Marrons — the marron people," she corrected, nodding yes while rejecting my pronunciation.

"*Les marrons* were the resistance. Our guerilla army."

"They drew plans of attack in their secret encampments, then rushed down to the plantations with machetes, with torches, with guns. Relentless, they came. Down from the mountains and up from the sand and swamp and they came and came. Attack, retreat. Attack, retreat. They did not sleep until this place—this stolen island of bones and blood— was purged of the White Death and the first slave republic in the history of humankind could draw breath!"

I'd been digging my fingernails into the palms of my hands. I pulled them out from beneath the duvet. Tried to uncurl them but my fingers were wrinkled, cold and locked up like chicken claws. Fradine examined them eyes narrowed in concentration.

"I think I have Reye's syndrome," I said by way of apology. "It's not contagious or anything. It just looks scary,"

"Reye's syndrome? Oh dear," she said. "Your fingers are cold, true," Taking both my claws into her own soft, warm hands, she rubbed them gently. Tendons relaxed and blood began to flow again. "What is the idiom— I used to know it—cold hands, warm heart?"

"I thought Henri Caesar was a pirate," I said, stretching my fingers experimentally. It was like she'd oiled all the little joints.

"Yes, he became a pirate! While slaving in the mill he dreamt of the sea. And he dreamt of treasure and riches of all kinds. Where are we now? It is 1805. The revolution was all but won! Henri *La Scie* and his comrades-in-arms had secured for themselves a small but seaworthy vessel. In it they joined the Haitian marine forces patrolling the north-west coast.

"Napoleon's crew?"

"Yes, that's right — you do know a little history! Yes, even after that treacherous little Frenchman conceded they had to be on constant lookout. The Eurins had no honor, and could never be trusted to keep their word. Anyway, Henri and his men joined the marine patrol and one day Henri saw a strange ship through his binoculars. It was not a battleship, however. It was a slaver! It was the Mahogany Queen, en route to Jamaica and full of African slaves and now? Blown off-course. It was very bad luck for the captain and crew to be stranded in free Haitian waters. Henri La Scie and his mates set upon the ship and … that was that!"

Fradine clapped her hands together.

"What did they do? What happened?" I said.

Terrible carnage. Nothing to smile about, even now. Suffice it to say that Henri The Saw was thirsty for revenge. He had already carved up the body of Dinclinson, the family Arnaut, and countless others. But the more blood he tasted, the more blood he craved. His blood-lust was real—it was in his DNA, after all. But that was but one small part of his true character. Deep in his young heart, more than battle, Henri—like his dead father—was a gentleman who admired a gracious, peaceful and refined life. He was a philosopher and a connoisseur. The Old Black Ones say this: The next day was Sunday, and Henri told his crew to bring their families and dress in their best clothes. And Henri had cooked for two days. Such rich smells emanated from the ship's galley! Spices and shallots and sea vegetables and fish eggs and meat.

"He ordered the table set, and candles lit, and the people feasted. They drank wine and rum and they laughed and told stories.

"But the party was not meant to last, for Henri and his crew soon set sail again, and they would be gone for months and months.

I said, "It must be a little scary, though. To go inside a slaver like that. Even if it's all remodeled."

Said Fradine, "Initially, yes. For you, certainly. There is an uneasy feeling one must pass through. But once you do so, you feel so much better! You will see. And anyway that is all in the past! And surely we can forgive what has passed. It's getting late," she added. "Both you and I should sleep,"

"Forgive and forget," I mumbled this mindlessly and with some difficulty. My tongue felt thick.

"Hein?!"

I startled. Told her I didn't know why I'd said that, I wasn't thinking it just came out. But Fradine was standing up now, glaring and sarcastic. "Forgive, yes of course, mais oui! After all, we are good Catholics, at least in part. That being said, I'd no sooner hang the Eurindigenous symbol of torture and suffering from my wall than would I hang a … a grinning death head!

She went on. Forgive and forget! I do not think you are half as simple as the words that come out of your mouth sometimes. We *did* forgive. And then we forgave and still we are forgiving and forgiving, it is an attenuated process. But to forget? Now wouldn't we look foolish! Our lives are spirals — not lines, konpronne? The past is as relentless as the future. Yes, we are optimistic! But at the same time, we are reasonable. It would be unreasonable for us to ignore the repeating pattern. We have learned to accept what we cannot change and sometime in the early aughts — I was in school then — the Old Black Ones came to a realization: We cannot change the collective nature of those who would pray to Dinclinson. We are banging the head against the wall. So let us think like lawyers and the immediate solution becomes clear: We can extract payment. You see the difference? In your country you say, 'Here are the receipts! Here are the records to prove my claim. You owe us now reparations.'"

"Reparations," I repeated.

"Reparations can be paid at such time that the perpetrator wishes to atone. However! He must himself desire. So what we have developed is a stop-gap policy of containment, paired with a weekly flesh tribute system. Like the ancient Greeks! And although I can no longer call myself a Catholic, the Old Testament is powerful and it does speak of a pound of flesh for a pound of flesh, c'est vrai.

My fingertips started shriveling back up and I was not sure I heard right. She misread my expression and hurried on.

"Ouais, ouais, it is not a perfect system. It is far from perfect but it has helped ease local tensions, making it possible for everyone to feel more secure. Of course les blanc—our Eurindigenous foreign visitors—they do understand that there is a small degree of risk involved but doesn't that just add to the...how do you say...the spice of travel and adventure? Like she says on Gracious Living, are you familiar? Have you seen the HelloCast withNicole—no matter. She says we must step outside our safety zones, psychological and otherwise, to cultivate wonder.

"So Café Dinclinson—" I was thinking of the white tourists, the odd homogeneity.

"Listen. In college I did a year abroad, you know, and while I was there The Old Black Ones formed an LLC and bought the remains of The Mahogany Queen. We were all so excited. The renovations took forever. When they finally opened for business the rumors began. They said the floating restaurant served white human flesh! Haiti's Tourism Ministry went crazy and launched a campaign to stomp out the gossip. Still, even today there are people who say that although you will not find it on any printed menu, human-flavored cell meat can be sampled on board. This is demonstrably false. Human-flavored meat is just as illegal in Haiti as it is in the United States and Europe and the Old Black Ones would never have it! Do you understand? Comprendes-tu? *konprann*, mam'zelle Charlotte?"

I did understand. I was sitting up now. Sitting up and peering through the shadows cast by the candle. Propped up on my elbow I stared into her face without a drop of self-consciousness and, serenely, she regarded me. Candlelight caught the silver springs of tinsel in her hair and her skin glowed. And she was holding something out to me and whatever it was I very much wanted. When I parted my lips to say so a cloud of hibiscus came out and I could see my words in it. My voice was not mine, it was dark-brown old fashioned French. It made a high peak arch before plummeting back down into the deepest purpling sizzle.

I cupped her hand in mine. She covered it and squeezed.

And in this oddly formal yet intimate way we held each other for what felt like a long time. I was smiling through the dark and nodding yes.

2.

The Savage Corner

Here is a candle, here is a chopper

Bea was vanished. I was lying in bed, passing each day just sort of luxuriating in my own body fluid when I remembered Bea and the kids. I woke up one morning and remembered everything so I flew down to the beach directly through the bush, never mind the road. I scrambled down like a goat, at times nearly parallel to the boulders, one hand for balance. Brambles sliced geometrics up and down my arms and legs.

The sandy lot was vacant, Bea's truck was gone. Her shack was deserted, windows smothered with sheets of plastic. The hand painted sign marking her Coin Sauvage was covered with official-looking sticker-tape reading INTERDITE! Forbidden. It was as if a bulldozer had scooped up the old bar stools, the battered half-functioning umbrellas, the sun-bleached hammock chairs, the random collection of books. I scrambled up the rickety stairs and, shielding my eyes, pressed my face to the glass above the door. It was too dark to see.

This all makes zero sense; I'm aware of that, thanks. But still. In the very best of circumstances it can sometimes be hard to know, for sure, what parts of reality are shared and what parts are meant to be private. I walked into the ocean, squishing kelp. Salt burned my little cuts and I figured that was good. Like antiseptic.

The trudge back up the road was sweaty and crippling. Clinging to my skirt were evil white balls. When I tried pulling one off, it dug its tiny hooked needles into my thumb and forefinger, latching them together like Velcro. It hurt when I tried to pull them apart. I tugged at the ball with my left hand and those two fingers got caught as well, if you can imagine it. I popped all four fingers into my mouth, soothing them with saliva. Tears mixed with sweat mixed with mucus. My every orifice like a faucet, purging whatever fluid I had left. I chewed my fingers free, spitting out vile chunks of prickly mush. Kept walking, coughing and spitting. An ankle strap had torn free from my sandal and whenever I forgot to grip the sole with my toes it flopped off and twisted around.

When I got to the gate my heart sank further because Fradine was standing there. *Like a gargoyle*. Then, remembering the bloody art installation I'd left in my bed I stumbled over my flopping sandal and she ran to me, alarmed. Put one dry palm on my forehead as I stood there, sinking.

She started in. Please tell me you didn't walk all the way to the beach!

You are bleeding! Are you crying? What did you get into now? Your face is red! Even if the sun is not shining you can still get sun poisoning, with your kind of skin! Don't you know that? Coralie said you went through the bush! Are you insane? Why do you want to hurt?

She grabbed my chin and brought her face close to mine. I stared back into her brown eyes for as long as I could. I felt she was filling me up with fear and confusion that wasn't my own. It feels ridiculous to say but I felt, from her, something close to love. Not quite, but in the neighborhood. Pity? Tears welled up and I wiggled out of her grasp, ashamed. *She wants me to go. She never signed up for Crazy.* That's what I was thinking.

But what I actually said was, "it's okay. Look, I'm pretty much healed and I can probably change my fligh—"

I think I just wanted to make it easier for all of us, but Fradine had a lot on her mind. She wailed in on me like, "What in God's name are you talking? You have been spending too much time alone, and I blame myself. What did you eat today? Nothing at all! I asked Coralie. Starting today you no longer have special treatment. No more trays to your bedroom. You are an honorary Masseaux, and you will dine at the table with us, starting with luncheon. P'tit Luc and Margot are on the veranda. You have just enough time to wash."

It would have been kinder to put me out on the street. I've recently developed this thing about sitting at the table with people. I hate it, I hate it. So I just stood there. Then she said, "Anyway, it's better for Coralie. Less work for her, *konprenns*?"

It was a sly, cheap move.There was no graceful way out and she knew it. I fake smiled and cursed her, telepathically, for using *my feelings for Coralie* like that when I'm already so deeply compromised. Still, I nodded and grunted my assent out of respect for skills. I slumped past here and hobbled up the stairs like the defeated teenager I never stopped being, I guess.

I had to make a plan. Had to throw sheets and towels in the bath with cold water, shampoo. Let the bloody mess soak, figure something out. But when I opened my bedroom door, shame turned to relief turned to guilt. My entire bed, mattress pad and duvet included, had been stripped and freshly made in crisp white cotton. The shelf in the bathroom was stacked with fresh new bath sheets and washcloths. A sweet bouquet of flowering herbs stood on the dresser. Coralie!

****

vintage Black Family Sit-Com title: ONE HAPPY GAY HAITIAN FAMILY

Episode Title: The Houseguest From the American South

Setting: Masseaux' veranda, 1pm. Lush, tropical mountain view. Formal table set for five.

Cast (in order of appearance)

Coralie 18. feminine vibe but slender masc. build.

Fradine Masseaux early 40's. Round, laughing, expressive, capricious, earthy-feminine pretty. Deep color, hair shorn. She is married to Big Luc.

Big Luc Masseaux early 50's. A serious, scholarly, masculine woman of imposing height, generous belly. Deep color. Puffy-faces. Wire-rimmed glasses. Very dense Salt-Pepper colored Afro textured like lambs wool.

P'tit Luc 28 is their ironically nicknamed (adopted) son. He's a transman with a Big head and a laughing, wide-open face covered in spots and freckles like an old banana. A chef at a family-style restaurant, he is engaged to be married to haughty Margot.

Margot 29, is a clever accountant at a modeling agency. Rich color, long throat, thick natural hair usually tied up in one of her trademark scarves. She is glamorous and stylish and accomplished – all the things Charlotte is not.

Charlotte Noa Tibbet 24, has the black hair and contrasting pale brown skin of many Louisiana Creoles. She is a guest of the Masseaux' B&B for two weeks. She has a lot of issues and problems. She also has a crush on Coralie. She will only be in Haiti for another week.

Charlotte is last to come to the table. When she enters, the two moms, their son and his fiancée are still standing. They were waiting for her to sit down and Charlotte's mood plummets. She feels out-classed and extra-vulnerable. Still, everyone is gracious and Fradine introduces her to Margot and P'tit Luc. Margot murmurs something to Charlotte in French. Charlotte, of course, does not know how to respond and, at any rate, is rescued by P'tit Luc's enthusiastic co-option of his mother's formal introduction.

P'tit Luc

It's a pleasure to meet you, Mamzelle Charlotte! Ouais, they told us you tumbled through the brier patches down Mont Masseaux! Excuse me for saying, Mamzelle, but you are not—how can I say this—not extraordinarily bright, are you?

P'tit Luc and Charlotte stare at one another in silence for a moment before they burst into laughter. Margot stares straight ahead.

CHARLOTTE (voice-over)

Margot dislikes me already. I can say this right off the bat because, historically speaking I've clashed with women like her. Think vintage urban sitcom and you get it. She's the Roxie Rokeresque/ strong.black.woman whose-sensibilities-are-often-offended, type. Crabs in a barrel, as they say back home. Kinda like my mother.

MARGOT

Non, non too,too early for me! Mais non, Mam'zelle. It's the sugar. Toujou avec la sucre, toi! You will not make me fat before my fitting!

CHARLOTTE (VO)

Predictable. Margot is the exact type to refuse something delicious for no reason than to show off and make me, the outsider, look bad. Just look at her. She won't try even one glass of Coralie's punch!

I didn't care for the familiar way she spoke to my Coralie. But I swallowed my pink rum punch—manfully I think—in two gulps. It was downhill from there.

CHARLOTTE (VO)

I finished my glass and then another as the Masseaux' went over details related to the upcoming "fitting." I am not a fan of weddings. By the time Coralie brought oufritters pink rum was talking.

CHARLOTTE (VO) I told them about the wholesale disappearance of Cape Town Bea on the Savage Corner and her wealthy, disappearing

Zulu.About precocious Denmark and fearless
Aristide—balustrade balancer extraordinaire.
About how un-welcome we were made to feel in
that weird little cordoned off beachside cafe.
About the malevolence in the proprietor's gaze and
how I could just tell he was a bigot.

(Direction)

Luc and Fradine exchange serious looks. P'tit Luc
is thoughtful. Margot seems matter-of-fact.
Charlotte is dominating the room with no sign of
easing up. The Masseaux are her polite but captive
audience.

CHARLOTTE (VO)

A cold breeze rushed over the veranda and I
stopped, shivering. How long had I been going on?
Too long, judging from their silence, and I didn't
even tell them everything. I didn't tell them the
monkey part — I'd swallowed that shock and hurt
deep down into my esophagus, out of reach. What
was the option? I guess I could have puked it back
up all over the table for the Masseaux' to share. I
just cut up my crepe into smaller and smaller
pieces. Kept doing it until both utensils scraped the
plate and Luc and Fradine winced. I'd crossed
some sort of line. It was quiet but for the sound of
Coralie running water in the kitchen. I panicked.

Okay Recalibrate. Minimize, parody, diffuse

CHARLOTTE

Anyway, Monsier Bigottry has an attitude
problem but the real tragedy here is that the
windsurf rental right next to his place—

CHARLOTTE (VO)

Wishing I had not ushered eurindigenous bigotry,
of all things, onto their beautiful veranda, I now
felt responsible for its exorcism. Which is the only
way I can explain why I then launched, sudden and
loud, into an extemporaneous soliloquy about
windsurfing.

CHARLOTTE

It would be like a dragonflies wing, skimming past
the reef to a world without words, with minimal
flesh—" when Margot, irritated, interrupted.

MARGOT

Cafe Dinclinson. That is Dinclinson's Cafe. How
did you get there? It is a good three kilometers!

CHARLOTTE

We just walked down the beach. It didn't seem that
far but we were looking for Ari, so

MARGOT

Actually we know of him, your Dinclinson. He came as a tourist years years back. Then we heard he bought that place—

P'tit Luc

Him! Everyone knows that one—

CHARLOTTE (VO)

I tried to change the subject by doubling down on my absurdity.

CHARLOTTE

I may never be happy until I, too, am one with the ocean!

CHARLOTTE (VO)

I actually said that shit. The Masseaux all stared – Fradine and Luc with bemusement, P'tit Luc with a bewildered expression and Margot with catty triumph.

Scene direction

Camera zooms out to show everyone at the table, then zooms back in to focus on Noa's face and skull. It zooms in, slowly, closer and closer. Background music is *merry melody* cartoon-loop insanity. HNow we can see the inside of her skull. Photographs of her mom with her grandmother, awkward school photos with glasses. Then with her grandfather at Christmas and at Easter. Sounds like a blender whirling around and around. You see her feeling left out, sitting uncomfortably on the Easter bunny's knee, little denim skirt riding up. Also in the blender are voices from the past, bits and pieces of conversations overlapping with her own voice from when she was a child ...

Grandfather VO

that child just doesn't look happy

Grandmother VO

You can handle your grandpere, cest bon ca pas non, Charlotte-Noa?

shrieking little girls VO

Go away monkeys! No Monkeys!

Teenage Charlotte's VO

Why did the monkey fall out of the tree?

Because he was dead.

Nicole VO

That's not funny Charlotte

(Stage direction)

When the swirling, loopy cartoon and whirling blender noise and the spinning kaleidoscope of images fades out, we go back to the dinner table where the Masseaux are eating and laughing. Margot, the bride-to-be, is center of attention. Charlotte is staring at Margot, seething. Proceeds to project her bitterness onto a laughing, joyous Margot.

CHARLOTTE (VO)

Your animus is showing, Queen. It's septic. People die from sepsis.You have your resentments I have mine but listen, Queen to Queen, we all know that yours matter most. I bow to your superior pain but I didn't ask to sit here so take it up with Fradine. I don't have to be nice. I am not nice. I am a big yellow mulatta-monster and, for now at least, a captive audience for your hate parade. It takes two to fucking tango and you, Mam'zelle Blacker-the-Berry, you are all about the lead.

direction

Coralie clears the table.

CHARLOTTE (VO)

Fradine wondered, aloud, if I was a little bit

unstable. At least that was my interpretation of her next comment.

FRADINE

Maybe your experience with this, ah, Bea person was some sort of hallucination? Perhaps she came to you as a vision of what could be, to show you possibilities you had not considered. In that case, perhaps Bea is really a possibility of you?

CHARLOTTE VO

Resentment tightened my throat.

CHARLOTTE

Bea is a Eurin. I have 56 points.

CHARLOTTE VO

My jaw felt tight and my words seemed to come from my gut, bypassing my brain, shooting through a hole in my neck like those old Pez dispensers. Disproportionate anger, for sure. Anger I had no right to carry. Tears welled, Blinding me. They were all looking at me. I excused myself from the table.

Later that night came a knock at the door, then pressure on the end of my bed. A hand on my forehead and for a thrilling half-second I thought it

was Coralie. It was Fradine and I burrowed my
face into the pillow.

FRADINE

How are you feeling?

CHARLOTTE
ridiculous, thanks.

Fradine

This has been a most difficult trip for you, I'm
afraid.

CHARLOTTE (VO) Fradine ignored the noises I
made into the pillow and nudged me to move over.
Surprised but pleased, I wiggled over to make
room. She struck a match over a candle attached to
the iron work on the headboard. With a pillow
against the wrought iron she settled back to talk
story.

3.

Blood Bed

Charlotte gains and loses time

The screeching howl in your throat is the same howl through both ears as you hurtle towards earth —still buckled to the seat of your aircraft. Or maybe you wake from a terrible dream to find your enormous pregnant body squeezed into farrowing irons in the bowels of a North Carolina pig factory.

Both scenarios are fair examples of Nearly Indescribable Horror because in both cases the victim understands—with every cell in her body—that there is no hope. When it comes to horror, significant elevating factors include duration and something else. Something that has to do with all that's in your head. I think the word is agency. From there we arrive at three possible outcomes: Death, followed by endurable and unendurable. With endurable horror you can see the possibility of a less terrible future.

And here's something else, related though. Say you decide to put your festering issue—that fucked-up memory, your bellowing tooth, your teratoma—into the hands of a trained professional. Things might not work out because, you know, sometimes they don't. But taking action feels better than just watching life happen to you. Worst case scenario you die but you take the leap anyway because sometimes there's no choice. You have to make yourself trust people. Not all people, but maybe one or two people. And although your eggs are all in one basket, at least you have your own basket. Coralie! I know I'm not making much sense but there is something here I am trying to put my finger on. It has to do with the relief of release. The release that follows surrender.

Surrender is a word worth sucking on and it's not inherently negative. I had my wisdom teeth extracted when I turned fourteen. That's just what they did then. Then came multiple fillings and a root canal. It's hard for you to imagine because your pretty teeth are so perfect, Coralie. But every year brought more decay until the rotting pulp of each molar was replaced with resin composite. This was all before bone cell regeneration. This may feel like a digression but it's all related, I promise you, Coralie. And I'm circling back around now because maybe surrender is just another word for trust.

Trust maybe, or faith. Faith is a cringy kind of word, I know, but right now it fits. Here's the reality: An oral surgeon—a disinterested professional—goes over your X-rays and all. After assessing the situation and setting an appointment, this lady, this doctor, has zero interest in assigning blame so if some dickhead tries to persuade her to not help — like "look her teeth are fucked-up due to her own filthy habits so let her suffer," she would say to them, whose fault this is not our concern, thanks for your input though! And you can probably trust her.

Now imagine you're tilted back in the robotic dentists' chair. Plastic clamps digging into your gums, lips spread wide open. Operating theater lights glaring into your cavities. Teeth, tongue, tonsils—all your insides turned out, exposed. Glistening mucous membranes on display. Different kinds of residue, all of it revolting. Biological evidence of short-cuts taken, fucks not given, weaknesses indulged. Time slows to a crawl and you can't help but absorb what you are certain is judgment. These doctors are tight, brisk, young, efficient. They have it together and they are glad they are not you but try not to think about that and you will, most likely, get through it. And when you get through it I can almost guarantee that your first breath of free air will taste like grace. Such grateful relief because you've been granted another roll of the dice, a fresh plate at the table, one more life or maybe eight more lives. There is no telling.

*****

A-vort-e-ment is Haitian French for abortion. Avortement sounds better, more dignified. The syllables have a (matter of fact)mouth-feel and repeating the word as I crawled back to the Masseaux', on my belly, like a snail. I squish-squished out the Clinique du Femmes and got halfway down the blistering pavement before my hot-pink Autocar pulled up alongside me, chirping: "Mam'zelle Charlotte to Maison Masseaux! En yva!"

The door slid open as my knees began to wobble, buckling in under a wave of gratitude. The locks clicked, the windows tinted dark, and I was in safe and headed home.

It was so good to see you there, Coralie. At the gate, perched up on the rock wall. I didn't recognize you at first; you were so beautiful in the sun. I saw a young girl, not at all developed so under fourteen or fifteen. Skin glowing, all but your face, enshadowed by twin afropuffs.

From the frog's eye vantage point afforded me from the autocar I could see all of you at once, and in that moment you appeared an idealized version of yourself. A sprite or a fairie, from the future and the past. You were cradling a small brown hen. Her feet hung down motionless as you stroked her head.

You put her in the basket so gently. I hope you know that I meant it when I offered to help you bury her. I hope you know that, at the stone stairs, when you gave me your arm, I didn't mean to lean on you so hard. I was triggered by your flesh and I leaned into that memory.

Coralie's arm was strong like KJ's arm was strong. I let myself believe that it was she, and that feeling was such a relief. I collapsed into her left shoulder and chest with a Dorothy Dandrige-level swoon. Coralie stumbled back under my sudden weight and if we hadn't started grabbing at each other we'd have been sprawled out on the gravel. But I grabbed and held on; turned into her flat chest. It wasn't flat like Matthew's, it was more broadly fleshy beneath her cotton dress. And when I turned to look into her eyes, already crinkling up with giggles, I could also see, to my astonishment, that she was hardly young. She was probably older than me, maybe in her thirties, and then we were both laughing and I remember wondering if things were finally all starting to make sense.

There is so much dark red blood. A rich, grim internal color they used to call ox blood. What I want to describe is an abundance of blood, a surplus of blood, a steady stream of tomato-red blood headed for a deep forest pool of blood and I am fascinated. Some of it soaked through my sanitary diaper shorts and when I woke up at some godless early morning hour I had to peel it off in strips, like flesh. It did not hurt but I cried anyway. Then sprayed off in the tub and wrapped up in one of Fradine's luscious bath sheets. Crawled back into bed without remorse because Fradine does not like me.

She never did, and maybe it's a creepy voudoun thing or a creepy Catholic thing but most likely it's not even that deep. No more than that persistent punk-ass bitch nemesis of Negro Society. Thinking back I'm sure I sensed something . . . I don't know. Something penetrating from her gaze. Appraising. That is a thing that exists whether or not I foul her nice sheets in embryo juice, so. In other words, if in fact she has a problem with my relative surfeit of melanin, well. It's not as if not bloodying the bed was going to make a difference.

A soft knock at my door and I straighten the duvet to cover the blood. Subtle little Coralie has me on a root tincture regime. Our relationship is progressing nicely with my convalescence. We share an understanding and have developed a little ritual: I close my eyes and open my mouth like an Easter peep until her bitter-flavored astringent droplets shrivel up the skin beneath my tongue. Then she lies next to me, gentle like a cat, on top of the duvet but under the crook of my arm. I pull her in close and breathe in her hair. She asks if I remember my dream. I always do.

I was making my way through a bowling-alley sized platter of bone meat – buffalo-chicken wings – under the covers in a spacious hotel bed. Tearing it with teeth and fingers, gobbling it down, sucking on the bones, tossing them to the floor like a wild hyena. I licked and sucked at the knuckles, the soft white cartilage. Then the chicken wasn't chicken at all; too soft and rich with too much fat. The bones weren't right. When I held a greasy chunk closer to my eyeball I could see they were the bones of a very small human. A homunculus! Stomach bulging I swept the entire mess to the floor with satisfaction.

I was then aware of being watched, but I couldn't find my glasses. I sang out, "Whoooo isss iiiit? Come iinn!" And there, standing at the threshold, was Matthew. It looked like he'd slept in his suit and his forehead was all creases.

He goes "What's the air on? It's hot as hell in here!"

And I'm like "Hey, how are you? I should've saved you s—"

He's like "It's so dark! Whattaya doing in the dark?"

I apologized; reached for the light by my bedside. A smear of reddish brown glistening against my arm and the metallic smell of blood.

"It's so dark!" I'd not before heard his upper register voice. He sounded frightened.

He squeakedYou're really dark, ya know that?"

I wanted to reassure him but was distracted, then captivated, by my reflection in his mirrored lenses. There were smears of blood on my mouth and nose and I laughed and laughed like a demon.

Coralie, frowning with concentration: "Are you certain the reflection you saw was you? Could it have been another woman's face in his lenses?"

I closed my eyes to think. And then, like an electric shock, I remembered Bea. What day is it? What

time is it? I gasp, startling her. Denmark and Ari!
Jumped out of bed and into the bath. Tumbled down
the path to the road to the beach parking lot.

4.

Welcome to New Haitians

The island bubbles with all kinds of life

There's Charlotte at the Port-au-Prince baggage claim, sweaty and panting in long sleeves and vinyl boots, struggling towards the exit with thrift store luggage. She wills herself forward, following musical GloTiles toward what seems to be a dead end. Stands before a wall of starry blue-green seaglass for the ten-second body scan before the wall parts into halves. As they do, a blast of hot air nearly brings her to her knees. At the same time a taste spreads over her tongue—thick, like overripe bananas, and clinging, like Easter lilies left standing too long. Yellow pollen dusting off everywhere.

She scans AutoDrive windshields and locates her reservation: Mme Charlotte a Jacmel. It's a hot pink three-seater—Matthew's sense of fun. She holds her up her wrist so that her watch faces the windshield. It glows green. "Bienvenue! Welcome! One way to Jacmal!" With new energy she hoists her bags into the open trunk. Folds herself into the generous back seat, squeezing legs to chest like an overgrown fetus. Doors slide shut and autoloc as HelloCast audio welcomes her to New Haiti in crisp standard English peppered with just enough African-American Vernacular to make one feel seen. There once was a time when that would have annoyed her, but not now. It was a nice feeling.

If this is your first visit to our little country, welcome home! And if you are one of our return visitors, welcome back!

You might find this hard to believe, little sister, but less than fifty years ago this green-glowing cityscape looked very different. The capital city was a war zone. The twentieth century was, as you might already know, a most difficult time. It was a time of pain and anxiety for the children of the African diaspora and of the global First Nations in general, but observers say that it seems that the Haitian people suffered disproportionately. True, we did heroically and repeatedly beat back the Eurindigenous slaver-aggressors, but when we realized that international communications had been co-opted, we struggled mightily in virtual isolation from our would-be allies.

Happily, those struggles are now in the rear-view and our tears have become tears of joy!

Today it is New Haiti's honor to represent nations

of the Caribbean, Central American Antilles and Caribbean Sea-facing South America in the United Nations . . .

Charlotte listens as she sleeps.

When people first think of Jacmal, they often think, "beach!"

There is good reason for this . . .

But do not let your enthusiasm make you blind to the many cultural attractions. The Big Puppet Theater, for example, will feature the Legend of Black Caesar for the rest of the month!

Haitian drumming for beginners at the music hall, text 411 for detailed information. Horticulturists will be interested in the Black Orchid forest nursery, but please do not attempt the self-guided tour. These rare Haitian orchids, world-renowned for their inner throats of indigo, must not be disturbed in any way. Tickets are available for a nominal fee.

Charlotte is awake when the tint on the windows lifts and the car comes to a stop.

Bienvenue and welcome to Jacmel! Bienvenue a Maison Masseaux! We have arrived!

Both doors slide open but Charlotte is mesmerized. The house is like a mansion, a magnificent ruin. A faded, haughty wreck of crumbling stone and wood, climbing with vines and waist-deep in rocks and thorny, flowering brush.

"Bienvenue, mademoiselle!"

Charlotte shrieks. Recovers.

"I did not mean to startle you! I am Coralie—" A slender girl leans in to peck Charlotte's cheek. Charlotte tries to reciprocate but moves to the wrong side and their foreheads collide. Coralie swallows a giggle as Charlotte tumbles over herself, ridiculously. Characteristically.

"Fradine and Luc will be happy to meet you," she adds, selecting the heaviest of Charlotte's two bags, one of which she swings easily over her shoulder and trots up the path towards a side entrance. Charlotte struggles behind.

Charlotte's bedroom is a study in white – white

Haitian linens, cream-colored plaster walls. One tiny window, and when she wakes in the morning there is a view of the sea. She stares out the window for hours. Pretends not to hear Coralie's soft raps at the door. Charlotte never eats breakfast.

It is close to noon when she makes it downstairs to meet Fradine and her wife.

"Your father called several times," this from Fradine, lips pinched in matronly disapproval. "You did not let him know you'd arrived last night, and parents cannot help but worry. I say this to you as a parent."

"My fath–?" Charlotte breaks off, realizes she must mean Matthew. A sly look passes over Fradine's face as she continues.

"So your bill is paid – for three full weeks," Fradine stares with open distaste at Charlotte's braless bosom. "He also transferred some extra for incidentals." The fog dissipates and Charlotte stiffins. Crosses one arm and then the other over her abdomen, as though putting on armor. You're enjoying this.

Smiling, Fradine looks away, triumphant. "We did try and wake you. He had a meeting. Very busy man. I had to give him a rough idea of what your expenses might be."

Charlotte's cheeks burn and she turns to go.

"Okay, sounds good,"

"Quoi? Eh bien, it really didn't feel like my place, but he could not reach you. Maybe while you are here you can update your watch? Or perhaps buy new?"

"Okay. I'll look into that. Thanks." I see you, auntie.

5.

Brown Recluse

Ahimsa fail

It's a long, sweaty stumbling walk down the rocky footpath and Charlotte is miserable until she passes under a tree full of mangos, nearly ripe. She stoops to pick one up from the ground one side is nearly hot to the touch, the other side cold, bruised and split open, juice oozing out. Charlotte sucks and chews on sweet-tart skin and flesh as the path widens and widens. The rocky sand turns to asphalt. Smells of hot, gooey blacktop thick with salt and the pounding of the surf. A dumpster and a few old cars in a sandy lot is all that separates her from the sea.

A rusty yellow pickup takes up more parking space than might be considerate. Loaded down with mango crates it squats in the blacktop. A pair of children—two dark-brown, skinny, yelping, shirtless children–gallop across its length, over the hood, down the windshield and back the other way, leaping over crates. Someone is going to get injured. Charlotte leans against a stack of sand encrusted wooden pallets and lights a cigarette in an effort to smoke the sticky sweet from her tongue.

She feels she is being sucked down. Sucked in. Like a doomed creature in a pit, the tar rising higher. "Tar Baby!" she thinks, and wonders over the phrase. Suddenly overwhelmed with heat and thirst. Heat steaming up from the pavement. Someone's going to get hurt, she is thinking. Come on, where are the parents.

"Coconut cream ready! Shave ice!"

The children freeze.

"Who wants shave-ice? Anyone?"

They leap from the pickup into the sand and around the corner, out of sight. They didn't go far, though. She can still hear their shouting. Charlotte puts out her cigarette and follows, guided by their noise, without a plan.

"Bonjou Mamzelle!" A wooden shack on stilts oversees what appears to be a small beach bar.

"You are ready for a mango-coconut cream?"

A hand-painted sign reads Le Coin Sauvage.

"I can give you with rum or without?"

It's really just a few stools on a crumbling slab of cement.

"Vien vite Mamzelle!"

The proprietress, a sturdy white woman with bleached-out hair, is waving both arms and calling out. Charlotte glances behind to make sure before approaching.

"With rum or without?" she repeats.

Charlotte hesitates. "With? With rum, I guess."

"We have a place for you here!"

Charlotte's place is on a stool between the two children, who are by now deeply involved in coconut cones of their own.

"You do not speak Kreyol?"

"A little bit. High school French. I understand more than I can speak."

"You are American, yes, I can tell. You have family on the island?"

Charlotte shakes her head.

"Do you want a family? I know of a very cute girl and boy, they might be fo–"

"Maman!"

"She doesn't mean it, Ari."

"This is Denmark and Aristide,"

Eyes on Charlotte's every swallow. Denmark eats carefully, with a spoon, while Ari is content to finger paint his bare chest and thighs with sticky white coconut cream.

Bea chatters—the adult-length surfboard upon which Ari can nearly balance, Denmark's budding career in musical theater.

"A singer and an actress, c'est pas vrais, Angelique?"

Denmark rolls her eyes.

"She's trying out for the lead in a musical. It's called The Wretched. Do you know it? "

Charlotte does not know it.

A New York director will bring his troupe down for the winter, Bea says. All of the children's roles will be played by local kids. "It's an old French story," she went on. "It was originally called . . .Les Misses – non – Les Desmoiselles?" Bea is uncertain.

"Oh wait – Les Miserables, right?"

"That's it! Denmark knows most of the score, but I can't make much sense of it–"

"I kinda remember now. We read it in high school."

"Excellent! So you can tell us then – what it is about?"

"A man steals bread and goes to prison. He gets out, maybe he escapes. I forget but he gets rich. Then he goes searching for his little daughter."

"Where was the momma?" Bea asks, with an anxious look.

Charlotte is uncertain.

"Where was the little boy?" screeches Ari, now standing on his stool.

"I don't think there was a little—" but Aristide leaps into the sand, landing on his hands and knees. Goes tearing down to the water's edge in his dirty lime green shorts. Bea is unconcerned.

"So you don't have any kids?"

"No! I mean, no."

Bea arches one brow. "You're good with kids, but?"

"I haven't re—"

"I can't pay you regular, but you don't have to go back to that creepy old house, you know. You can stay here as much as you want, and if you can keep company with the Friday and Saturday nights, and maybe Thursday, I can take this gig.

Charlotte smiles.

"Vraiment? Perfect! Listen, there is a show at the sea wall tonight. It's going to a good show – lots of tourists. I need to open the bar in an hour, but if you don't mind sitting with the kids it will be one less worry for me . . .

Charlotte is nodding and smiling.

"They're doing Henri Caesar. You can sit on the sea wall –it's the best view! With the moon and all." And then she was gone.

"Boring old Black Caesar," this from Ari, who has returned from his journey to the sea.

"You're boring!" Denmark shoves her fingers into his temple.

Charlotte settles on the wall, one skinny, salty child on either side. The moon glowed like an enormous orange, just beyond the Grande Pier. Drumming, music, and then came the puppets.

Monster-sized shadow puppets! The five sails of a clipper ship tossed by the tide. Gun and cannon fire booms and pops what looks like starbursts in the night sky. Through the darkness one can barely see the lithe bodies of the puppeter actors – seemed that the very smallest puppets needed a crew of at least four black-clad puppeteers. Charlotte is entranced. So absorbed, in fact, that when she reaches across Denmark to relieve Aristide of the communal coconut milk, there is only empty space.

"Where's your brother?" Charlotte grips Denmark's arm.

"Maybe he's swinging from a tree," she says. "You're hurting!"

But Charlotte tightens her grip and pulls the ten-year-old to her feet, drags her down the boardwalk.

"Think, Denmark! Would he go?"

Denmark shrugs and sighs. Together they race down the beach through the darkness — the only lights twinkled over booths selling box dinners and ice cold Haitian beer. Charlotte can no longer see – her eyes have flooded. She trips over her feet when Denmark stops cold, digging in her heels. She jerks on her wrist with her free hand.

"There he is!" Pointing up. There he is, maybe fifty feet away, his short legs beginning where the heads of the mall crowd end. Arms outstretched, his little brown feet grip a guard rail banister supporting a velvety rope, squaring off a beachside cafe. Most of the tiny tables are occupied. Weirdly enough, every patron looks white. Charlotte ducks beneath the rope and weaves through the tables, but before she gets to him she is startled by a man's bellowing voice. "Get him down! This is not a playground!"

"What do you think I'm doing?" Charlotte's cheeks burn.

One agile foot in front of the other, Aristide glides, upper body still but for the rise and fall of his breath.

"Ici un plage privee, private beach. Tu comprends? Not the zoo!"

Ari looks down to see Charlotte's petrified face through the sea of Eurindigenous faces and he grins, his joy complete. Complete as the laughing trickster loa.

"Excuse me! Excuse me! S'il tu plait, mam'zelle! Please can you get your little monkeys and go!"

A grip of nausea, then. As if someone had grabbed inside to twist her internal organs.

Denmark says, "Better monkey than a dick-lick-son!"

The patrons look away.

There's Charlotte in motion, three long strides with arms extended. She snatches giggling Ari, arms around his ankles. He collapses over her shoulder chanting "Funky Monkey Dick-lick-son!"

Denmark is on a roll: "Goodbye Dick-lick-son! Eat shit, Penis Breath!"

The man wheezed. "You should know to stay out from here!" Face red and twisted he yells after them in French. Most of it she can't understand, but she gets the message. "Let him fall . . . face cracked open . . .like an egg!"

Which hits Charlotte in a strange way, like when she slammed her shin really hard and the pain radiated up through her skeleton and she laughed. Laughter was gurgling up in her throat. She could have curled to the sand in hiccuping giggles with Ari. Except Aristide was no longer giggling—he was screeching like a parrot.

"StupidassmonkeyassAri," Denmark grumbles.

And then it is raining. Warm and dense rain speckling the sand and pock marking the ocean. The sky is as black as the sea. Charlotte, Denmark and Ari join hands and run through the storm back to Bea, who was closing up the bar.

"Perfect timing!" was all their mother said, to Charlotte's relief. and they climbed the wooden stairs into their home. They lived right there.

"No lights again," this from Denmark, with a performative sigh.

"No lights, ma pauvre. Vrai désolée." Bea flicks a lamp switch back and forth, experimentally.

"No lights, no bath!" chants Aristide.

Denmark sings: "Please do not send me out alone! Out in the darkness on my own!"

Bea responds through the dark, her voice nearly as clear but deeper in the chest:

"Now ferme la! Or I'll forget to be nice!"

Charlotte catches herself humming along and wonders where that came from. The little house rocks and groans and squeaks in the wind.

The storm thins into a patter on the tin roof. They crowd into the covered deck. Charlotte settles into a moldy-cushioned rocking chair, Aristide and Denmark sprawl on the rug to eat the contents of a boxed dinner. Bea pours two goblets of sweet yellow sherry. Charlotte curls both hands around her glass, and this is what she learns.

The childrens' father was an exchange student from Johannesburg, Bea was the eccentric daughter in her white liberal Cape Town family. She had left South Africa for no good reason when they met up in Hokkaido. When they first met they mountain climbed together. They dressed in Polartec and

Gortex and mountain climbed. He was a purist; extreme in all things. But she is romantic and will never give up hope, she said."It was me who could open up his heart."

In the end he went back to South Africa to work for his father. Bea will never return. The kids don't remember their dad, and they will always have a home in Haiti. Haiti is the best place in the world to raise children.

"Here you have everything," she says. "A progressive people's government, the best in the Americas!"

Charlotte imagines a dark brown island baby, puffy face lit up with a frizzy gold aureole of hair. Pictures herself in the market, big-breasted and bare-footed buying rice and peas on credit. Carrying them to the sea to wash in the early morning hours, while it is still quiet, before the tourists tumble in.

"I fell asleep too," says Bea, waking her up. "Island rain is like a drug."

There's Charlotte, blinking up at Bea who'd changed into a sea-foam colored gown, with sequins and just one sleeve. It was a little tight but they got it zipped up, with teamwork. Bea sucks in, Charlotte squeezes both sides together, Denmark pulls gently on the zipper. Aristide provides bird calls from his perch above a broken refrigerator. Next Bea applies lipstick and glitter while Charlotte and Denmark watch, entranced. White heels and a matching bag follow.

"How do I look?"

"DEELIGHTFUL!" Aristide howls, this time from the crawl space beneath the hall closet.

"It's an easy job," she says. "These hostess bars are all over. You just pour drinks and smile, sing karaoke, help them to drink more. They're all rich businessmen, lonely for home, missing New York, Shanghai, London you name it . . ."

Then she is gone, and Charlotte and the kids sit on the porch looking off at the place in the road where they'd last seen her taillights. Ari curls into a ball on the floor, his breath slow and even. Charlotte eats all six strawberry mangoes that stood ripening in the windowsill, one after the other. Denmark doesn't want any.

"Don't stuff," she protests. "It's not good to stuff!"

"You're right," says Charlotte, licking juice from her wrist.

"They fall off the tree when it rains. If you stay here with us, you can eat them every night."

"Every night? That's quite an offer!"

Denmark watches Charlotte's face, brow furrowed.

"I'll have to give an offer like that some serious thought," Charlotte continued, grinning. Then, remembering, she stiffens. "I have to get to an appointment tomorrow morning, first thing."

"You should write it down," says Denmark. "If you write it down you won't forget."

Movement across the top of the wall. A tumble of fuzz near the ceiling. Charlotte blinks, gets slowly to her feet, breath in her throat. It stops moving. Charlotte is frozen in place. With increasing dread she counts five, six, seven legs before it scrambles to the corner near Bea's old chifferobe. Disappears into the wood.

"Just a cane spider," Denmark sighs. "They don't bite you if you let them alone."

"It could be a cane spider, that's true," Charlotte tries to swallow through her tightening throat. "But what if he is a...uh...a venomous Brown Recluse?"

"What if she is a Charlotte? Charlotte's Web Charlotte? What if she has babies to save?"

That stings. Charlotte still frozen, considers. But there is nothing left to consider and she is rarely been so focussed. It might reappear if she waits. She waits. Then reaches for the knob and throws open the chifferobe door. There it is! Three feet from her face, legs splayed in eight directions. Fucker's nearly big as her palm. She springs back and the vibration sends it scurrying into the corner.

Next comes a high, thin voice and Charlotte is momentarily confused. But it was just Denmark, of course it was.

"Poor little thing. It just wants to get away." Denmark throws her arms around Charlotte's middle, pressing her ear into her gut.

"Umhum, " Charlotte wraps a protective arm around the child. The gesture feels natural, but before she can wonder over that, Denmark shifts her weight, jabbing her bony chin deep into Charlotte's solar plexus.

"I can hear you digesting," she says. "You ate too many mangoes and you ate them too fast."

"Has anyone ever told you that you have a very sharp chin?"

"You shouldn't stuff. It's not good to stuff, " she repeats, underlining her point.

"Your chin could be a lethal weapon. If you ever want to visit the States you'll have to get it registered."

Aristide snores. He sleeps on his belly, in the same

position Charlotte prefers. Flat like a frog, arms and legs sprawled.

Charlotte moves with precision. Tightening one arm around Denmark she slams shut the closet door, crunching the spider between plaster and wood. Opens the door and there it is, smashed flat like art. Denmark scowls. The warm, wet island wind blows in through the porch window, billowing up the tye-dyed curtain-sarong. It sucks back in, concave.

6.

Exodus

Charlotte's Diaspora Chart has 56 African dna points

The AmeriBank Pay Toilet between third and St. Marx is broke, so Charlotte stands outside that leather bar, bouncing from foot to foot. Come on little brah, a break! The bounce—boi swings his luxuriant faux—locs behind his shoulders. Looks above and through her and Charlotte knows what he's thinking.

Traitorous fuck! A tremendous spasm of will and her muscles cramp shut. Urine creeps back up a bit. Charlotte seethes, stares into his brown—green irides. They kaleidoscope with green and yellow dandelion flecks of bemusement.

"Is this funny? Am I funny to you?" She can smell her own breath; tastes like bile.

He points towards the brass letters above the door — QM/T*SS. Charlotte sounds out the acronym QueerMasc Transboi SafeSpace my cunt. Charlotte wills his eyes to meet hers, her blackening irides well on their way to what she hoped was a startling opacity.

Afraid of your fat yt daddy-boss and I should kick you in the neck. The door swings open, bangs against brick. A thick-set, pale-eyed ginger with elaborately sculpted facial hair appears, drawing on a pipe.

Charlotte turns away to study her burner. She isn't stupid. Takes a few steps towards the curb, as though suddenly preoccupied with a text. Prepared to leave another message she pushes redial, but Matthew picks up immediately. Charlotte's claws retract and she slumps against the building. Limp with relief so profound it feels like pleasure.

"Really? Wow. No kidding!" Friendly concern. "Huh. What are we going to do?" Matthew is a problem-solver.

"I'd like to see Tucson."

"Arizona? Huh. Well, I guess that semi-autonomous hippie region could be fun."

"Um." She doesn't mention the real draw — those giant cacti standing along the highway median like hitchhikers.

"They've got roadrunners too," Matthew is a mindreader. "But they don't look like the cartoon.

Small and dusty. Scorpions, big spiders. And doesn't it just stay hot? Like all year long?"

"I'm also thinking Oakland. Oakland has the ocean and everything."

"Sure, change of scenery. If I could just pack up start over I'd head for Kyoto. Or Haiti. Everywhere you go there's these gorgeous adverts for Haiti."

Haiti! She tries to imagine it. She has never seen clear blue water, warm and clean like a bath. Bamboo palms thick down trees. Talking birds and the Voudoun pantheon of human-sized lwa watching over, sometimes available for consult.

"Sure!" she snuffles, wipes her nose on her sleeve. "But my SCS is deep negative. Worse than last month, somehow."

"What is it?"

"Minus two."

"Minus—? How do you ev—" He stopped himself then. "I'll arrange it, okay? Consider it done."

"I'm sorry I—"

"Done. Not a problem."

A long pause. Too long, and she scrambled to fill it.

"Hey, I've been doing some research, and there is a chance it might not even be a fetus. Too early to tell but it could be some sort of hybrid tumor — a homunculus."

A pause after Matthew clears his throat. He will wait this out — whatever it is.

"Seriously, that's what they're called — homunculus. It's Latin for 'little man.'

More silence.

"It's kind of sex tumor and it develops hair and fingernails as it grows. Sometimes part of an eye or a tooth in random places. It's not even that uncommon!"

No response.

"I'm just saying that its a thing that exists. That can happen."

"Look, I gotta ask you," a jagged exhale. "What exactly were you doing all that time, all those times, in the bathroom?"

Studying my reflection in pink hotel lights. Wondering how it feels to be rich. Imagining my smiling cervix lined with teeth to welcome little fishes in. Like in the poem.

"Did you ever read 'Alice in Wonderland?' As a kid, I mean?"

"What?"

"I don't know. Nevermind."

"Look I have a meeting in five, so—"

"Yeah, me too. Talk later." She hangs up first.

7.

Chickenman

Elections have consequences

When Javanka Inc. took Cleveland, KJ called it a night. Which struck me as cynical and premature. And passive-aggressive so I didn't even turn around. Just stood there, blocking the gloscreen, chest tight. But when I sensed her attention settle and linger on the back of my heart – on that slight depression between my shoulder blades – a bubble of hope swelled up. And then there was nothing, just gone. I spun around as the elevator door sucked shut. She was up to bed and I hated her again. I hated each and every white bitch in the watch room, but most of all I hated her.

I pulled my hood all the way up and over, tried to clear the mucusy-bile in my throat. Boston fell, of course. Then Baltimore and Detroit and the little watch party was over. People blinked and flickered out like Christmas lights – three, two, and then just me, alone.

All along there were signs; some puzzle pieces seemed forced in. Even the truest of true believers could have read the signs but it still hurts to go on about it. So just this: When telebots scanned their faces – the winning team – I read shock, bewilderment, consternation. And then came triumph! The white light of triumph subsuming everything.

Hearing/not hearing the concession speeches I paced the watchroom; too wired to sit. Wide-awake and vibrating with anxious despair. And a loneliness that sent me stumbling from Sanger Towers onto west 67th towards Protestpark like a zombie. Seeking comfort, I guess, from proximity to strangers who looked the way I felt: Shell-shocked and mute. Mostly headed towards lights and drums. Parody puppets were setting up on stilts and globeams flashed our rage into the sky.

Watching US?

U we C

Axis of Au-to-cra-cy!

Licensed drummers banging and pounding. Coordination isn't necessary for large events anymore, not really. Beats are mixed and syncopated in the cloud; amplified back. You can just play from the heart. Anyone can. Just last week

I announced I'd put in for a drum license and KJ – or Katja, as she now prefers – said nothing. She didn't need to because her lip snailed up, exposing a tooth. A tooth of contempt!

Fear will never lead us (They will never lead us)

They will never know us (They have never known us)

KJ and I are registered activists for the Non-Human Animal Rights Collective, which is why we get to live in the Towers. Advocacy is exhausting work and I can never find time to think about much else. So it was weird when she started going on about the "poaching and co-option" of "real music." I can't say exactly when, but at some point last year she'd adopted this extracurricular outrage. It has become – outside of NARC – the only subject guaranteed to bring her from neutral to banshee. The general importance of it all isn't hard to grasp but I struggle to understand why all of a sudden she cares so damn much.

A few familiar faces in the park, KJ's people. I kept my hoodie up. Crowd was thickening but I just kept moving, kept pushing through. Didn't know what I was looking for until I saw them – a good-looking circle of Afrapunks. Art Academy folks, maybe.

Impulsivity is pretty much my brand, so I joined them.

The lead drummer was a sexy somebody. Shoulders rippling with natural muscle. Brown-blue sateen for skin. She felt me looking and flashed me a broad, cartoon wink before issuing the next call and I caught a rush of feels! Pushed back my hood and pulled my hair out. Only thing to make the moment more perfect would have been KJ's presence. Go ahead and push me down the chute and keep on climbing, girlfriend, I see you. I'll slide right out to here, into the cooler, hotter culture that was—after all—my birthright. My stomach flipped but I managed to join the response on beat. I was out of practice. It's like jumping in while the ropes are turning. I chanted louder, only to cringe at the tin-can sound of my own voice, weak in my ears. I glanced up but the drummer girl was looking in the other direction.

Tears welled up and I wiped my nose until my shirt-sleeve gloves were dirty and wet. Tried to focus on my youthful new friends but the tears kept coming. Their curiosity and pity kept them bubbling up. The drummer girl changed up the beat, the others caught it and drew closer in. Gently squeezed me from my spot, urging me, wordlessly, into the center. A circle of protection. I was embarrassed but mostly grateful. Seemed they'd adopted what I will now describe as a proprietary interest in my well-being. Their expensive contact lenses – Emoeyes they're called – glowed olive and hazel. Colors used to convey a kind of sympathy. A well-meant, if detached, acceptance.

But then I wasn't sure. I heard part of a joke that I didn't get. Then I lost the beat and when I did, I thought I heard them grinning. Yet when I searched their faces I read earnest, controlled concentration. Too earnest. Something dissonant and confusing until – eureka. They were protest voters! Of course they were. Their Emoeyes shone clear and dry – no tears for them. Only the satisfaction of the vindicated. And my presence was more than welcome, for I brought the authenticity. I was their stumbling, sobbing cautionary tale.

Seething, I faced the lead drummer. She gazed soberly into my fury, chanting. I willed myself to hold her gaze as the hazel in her irides darkened and widened. Then glossed into metallic reflection mode. Staring back at me was me – a broken puppet. Outdated, irrelevant, derivative and clinging. My chest tightened and I shoved out and away from her, away from all of them. Out and away from Protestpark. It was drizzling.

Headed south down Detroit Avenue without a plan. Rain falling at an increasingly aggressive angle. I walked faster, seeing little and retaining nothing. Half an hour later I stood in the belly of Free Trade Square, sheltered beneath the enormous half-moon awning of one of the monstrous new hotels. Etched onto the heated pavement was a nesting bird, head tucked under her wing. The irony-free logo for the Number One L'Hotel Double-Grand Lux, according to the signage.

The guestplease sensor must have been malfunctioning, because the glass doors parted as I approached. They spread wide apart with a swooshing sound of welcome and the scent of sandalwood. The radiant heat was deliciously warm on my skin. I stepped into the lobby and waited for the silent approach of the inevitable security bot. Nothing. Feeling reckless, I stepped into the glass cube elevator and pressed the top button for the Sky Lounge. It was as if that glossy luxury chain hotel – the exact sort of place I'd never thought to enter for any reason – had been waiting up just for me.

I certainly wasn't looking my best. Hadn't changed out of my jeans in days, and I was skinnier than most people find attractive. Hadn't brushed my teeth either, a petty act of defiance. KJ was a fanatic for clean teeth and had hers' scrubbed once a month by an obese hygienist. The first Wednesday of every month.

The Premier Envoy Sky Lounge was velvety and dark. The bartender glanced up to nod, preoccupied with his Gloscreen. He gestured towards the clusters of furniture arrangements, the overlapping Persian rugs sprawled under velvet corduroy chairs with generous arms and high backs. I found a place in the far back corner, where no one could sneak up behind me. An egg-shaped ottoman doubled as a gloscreen, and I did a little math. I had just enough credits for a single cannabis-spiked cocktail, which would have zero effect. But something thick and filthy-tasting could help a little. At least I could make it last.

I scanned the room: hardly anyone around – a few business-type suits huddled by the plate glass window. Three elderly ladies giggled at the bar over milky cocktails. Two round tables pushed together made the most noise – uninhibited tourists from the sound of it. Laughing and chattering in muffled Chinese. I took everything in and I liked it, all of it. My jeans and shirt were almost dry. A warm towel arrived, followed by small bowls of sugared ginger and tree nuts. I uncurled a bit more and settled in for some serious thinking re: KJ. Who was, I'd deduced, looking for a change.

I didn't need a third eye to see it coming. She'd wake up tomorrow and look at the bright side to all this waste and death. And how can on argue with the evergreen wisdom contained in the phrase "allowing space to process?" I know the truth: Katja is more than ready to reclaim her birthright, and by that I mean her relatively high position on the Golden Rope.

This is about to get childish but I need to state

for the record that we got together because she pursued me. And she did so, in part, because being together with someone like me made her feel-by contrast-even more pure. Pure and powerful. At some point it started feeling heavy, I'm thinking. And then exhausting: All the advising, empathizing, defending and explaining. The subsidizing. At some point she must have noticed a pattern of diminishing returns.

How to explain it. Like, a while back I caught her watching me eat leftover pasta with my fingers. I tried to make a joke but she looked away quick – not even a smile. And that —that right there —is sad, cruel irony. Because before we moved in I almost always ate with a knife, fork and napkin because that's all I knew. She's the one who likes to chew with her mouth half open. Point is, I was the one who adjusted to her.

All this sounds petty because it is. But petty and powerful are hardly mutually exclusive! Everyone says they want a better deal for everyone else. And yet! Who amongst us will be first to forfeit their place on the Golden Rope? It's an oily, slippery noose of Rapunzel hair and it's dangling over Molasses Swamp. Every single one of us clings tight to it because Molasses Swamp is not really molasses. It's a quick-sand tar pit full of bones and congealed blood.

I had to pull it together and I was thinking Tucson.

You can get paid to move there if you promise to work a certain kind of job and I could get in on this entry-level solar farm technician internship. There's a doc on HelloCast. It's boiling hot and you pay for water and you're surrounded by hatefilled Eurins but. A bunch of old-school lesbian hippies took control a downtown section a couple years back and they're actively recruiting. Rent is super-cheap. Also, Tucson is beautiful. It looks just like an old cartoon – roadrunners and coyotes running around. Giant cactus just standing there along the highway, arms stretched out like they want a hug.

Scotch was served in a heavy crystal glass—the most beautiful glass I'd ever held. A hundred little etchings made a prism from the jewel tones in the rug. I was captivated. So much so that I nearly missed his eyes flicker-focus-flicker in my direction. When he looked at me again I jumped, nearly spilling. I am easily startled.

He had a big jaw and a lived-in face. Early forties and Eurindigenous. Brown hair with gray all through it. Suit jacket still on, tie pulled loose. He looked expensive. He looked like a winner and as that last thought took shape I was overcome with grief. I squashed it down, pummeled it to malice. Sharpened my teeth and stared back, blackening and flattening my irides. He turned away and gulped his drink because you really don't need

Emoeyes to make a non-verbal point, just practice and focus.

Or not, because it didn't actually work. He made a quick gesture in my direction and just kept on conversating with the bartender. But then moving in my direction, the little clusters of furniture making it less than a straight shot. Which gave me just enough time to panic. I looked away, fumbled my glass. Hadn't expected agility from such a large person. But there you go – the easy unselfconsciousness of a lifetime of privilege. Would I mind if he joined me?

"Why, certainly!" I said, louder and heartier than anything that could pass for normal. "Have a seat!"

My fingertips were wrinkling up and turning a bloodless grey. They do that sometimes because of my heart murmur.

"Whattaya drinking?" He said it just like that, 'Whattaya drinking?' like in a film. Which meant, I realized, that he meant to pay! Not just the drink he proposed, but the one I was already half-through and I could have wept at my good fortune. He was certainly brave to go out of his way to sit with the patron most likely to be shot dead by an errant security bot. And yet there he sat, pretending this was normal (Are Cleveland winters always so balmy? Name's Matthew, by the way.) Chatting at me like to the sister of a good buddy while I inhaled the fragrance of a very fine scotch. Coated my tongue and teeth with silky peat, over and under.

"Hope you don't mind, but I upgraded your drink. Same maker, aged longer."

"It's lovely," I said.

"I'm serious about the weather, though. Just flew in from Anchorage."

"I guess it's warm, I don't know. I grew up down south."

He talked about scuba diving; he loved to scuba dive. I should try it if I ever got the chance, he'd seen such amazing worlds underwater. He liked to play golf (golf!) He liked to run marathons (why?) He traveled a lot but he didn't enjoy it. It could be lonely. Do I like to travel?

"It's good you've had the chance to scuba dive, while fish still exist, I

mean," I couldn't help it.

"Right," he said, nodding comfortably. "Illegal overfishing, it's just so short-sighted. I only buy organic fish. The sustainable, farm-raised kind," he added.

I'd been wondering if he might spring a fancy cell-shrimp snack so tried to stay quiet. I didn't want to fight. But duty called so I checked my tone and made ready for a sneak attack. "Fishing, as I understand it, involves a pole and a hook or maybe a net," I began.

"Yeah I grew up on the lake. Love it! You ever been to Lake Ontario?

I continued. "We've had zero fishing in this country for nearly fifty years. We don't fish, we war on fish. Death Trawlers controlled by satellite patrol the seas and crush-capture-maim everything swimming, floating or crawling in its path."

He picked up his drink, nodding. Put it back down without taking a sip.

"You have a point, there are some bad actors out there. But we did pass the Fisheries Ac—""

"Toothless," I said, irritable. My glass almost empty"Passed to make people feel better about doing what they've always done. What's the point of legislation without enforcement?"

We sat in silence until my stomach growled audibly. I cursed my lack of discipline—he'd never spring for food now. But what he said was, "You're probably right. Yeah, that seems about right. Hey, you at all hungry?"

He leaned over to activate the gloscreen.

I picked up my glass with fresh appreciation. Pretty soon he was on again, accepting my vague responses to his not-at-all intrusive queries. He ordered dumplings stuffed with cell-pork for himself and cell-shrimp cocktail for me. Responding to my uninspired "and yourself?" reciprocations with a generous level of thoughtfulness and detail. But as he went on about his career (frozen food), his personal life (married with daughters), my mind wandered and I felt myself sinking. There is shame when I say this, but I was tired of advocating.

Matthew believed himself good, so in an existential sort of way, he was. Objectively, of course, he is a well-paid player in Big Food's flesh trade. That's what KJ would say. She would tell him that in the time it will take to finish his fake meat, hundreds of thousands of non-human animals will have been tortured to death. And she would be right. But how to quantify evil? Evil, like cruelty, requires understanding. Surely.

"The best diving ever is off the north coast of Haiti," Mathew was back to travel and recreation. "Amazing shipwrecks, sure, but did you know they have the largest simulated Atlantic coral reef in the world?"

I did not know that. "You have to see the Caribbean. Have you had a chance to go?"

I told him I have no desire to travel. Which is the saddest sort of lie so I walked it back. "I mean, Cleveland is, pretty much, the center of the world, so—" I let my voice trail off. He held my gaze for an extra long moment. Then he laughed a big, round truncated ha!

Which filled my heart with gratitude because KJ never laughs at my jokes.

I once overheard her apologizing (for me!) to our downstairs neighbor. I only heard a little bit. She was saying, "so inappropriate. So not cool!" and then, "She can get pretty dark," Which felt racial, obviously.

The food was amazing. Maybe because I was starving, but it certainly soothed my rage. I asked Matthew something forgettable about his work, out of gratitude. Career talk (even if said career relies on the Bone Meat industrial complex) is terra firma for people like him. I realized he'd assumed that my area of concern was what HelloCasters still call v"The Environment." So he was talking up their Guiltless Real Chicken, genetically modified to not feel pain or fear. Which is a twisted concept, clearly. But it's also uncalled for, given the advent of cell meat and the fify other meat and egg options that already exist. I stared at the menu on the gloscreen; wondered if maybe he was fucking with me. I was finally feeling pretty good and I wasn't going to let him change that so I tuned him out.

Pulled my legs up under me and ordered another cell-shrimp cocktail.

"You still hungry?" he said, incredulous, "It's like you've never eaten before! Go on and eat, girl!"

I gave him the guilty-yet-adorable smile I save for special as he segued to global food culture. "Chicken, we've found, is both culturally specific and shape-shiftingly neutral," he began. "Everyone has a proprietary interest, and that's a plus! You have Chicken Kiev, Chicken and Dumplings, Chicken Marsala, Chicken yakitori, Kung p–"

I've seen video from inside Japan's chicken towers, and everyone knows how farmed animals are treated in Russia. But there I was, trying to enjoy a break from pain, and he seemed weirdly determined to not let that happen. "From eastern Europe to east Asia, awesome," I heard myself growl. "But how does that justify your glorified factory-farms? So what if they eat organic? It's still a life of tortu-"

"Nope. Never torture, ever. We only contract with certified GentleFinish producers. Finishing plants-"

Me: Slaughter plants!

Matthew: No issues with the word slaughter. It is, after all, what we do. But they are randomly inspected for adherence to various Harm Reduction protocols. But you can say slaughter. Life and death, killing, eating – it is the natural cycle of life-

Me: Natural? Can you think of a single example in nature that involves forcibly impregnating millions of female bodie–

Matthew: Now pigs are smart. You probably know that—you hear all kinds of anecdotes. But chickens . . .okay, they feel pain, but not like us. And cows, they have these bland expressions, don't they? I mean, I grew up on a farm, actually. I grew up with cows so I speak with some authority? Have you ever spent an hour with a cow? I mean, do cows even know what's happening? Okay, I can see you disagree. Okay. But you must – you do concede … Surely you will acknowledge that chicken cognition is somewhat limited?

He was making a joke and he needed me to smile. I sensed his need and I nearly obliged because I can be pathologically empathetic. A part of me really wanted to deliver. I couldn't, though. Not yet. "Look. Speaking as a darkie, I need to point out that similar arguments have been made about black and brown human animals, and also, when it's convenient, white poors. All this in a continuing effort to rationalize social inequality."

I knew my lines by heart, which was good because I was drunk. Next thing I remember is Matthew leaning in, speaking in a low, intimate tone, about cream. He did enjoy a little light cream in his coffee, he said. But only the kind from pasture-raised cows. Matching his tone, I channeled Eartha

Kitt and whispered that I'd drink urine from a public toilet over a tablespoon of "light cream" any day of the week.

He laughed and signaled for another round. I crumpled back into the velvet, looked away. Sunk deep into the memory of a field trip to an "authentic family dairy farm" a couple hours bus ride from St. Paul's. The farmer, a pale-eyed woman with a beaten down look, gathered us sixth graders around a solitary cow on a cement block. The cow's name was Mama.

"When I was you-alls age we always had a negra. Did all the milking by hand," she said, gazing wistfully, reminiscently, over our heads. Mama's distended teats were metal-clamped to plastic tubes, wired to an electric box. Directing our attention to the calibrator, the filthy-minded old cracker flicked a lever. The motor groaned as watery milk drained from Mama's udder.

"If she's a mama, where are her babies?" I don't think I asked out loud. What I do recall is that although I was at least a year out from needing a bra, I stood there hunched over, arms crossed tight over my chest. My red horn-rimmed eyeglasses fogging up. Thicker and thicker until I couldn't see anything at all.

"I think I know how you feel, actually." Matthew nodded. "Milk allergy is no joke. My youngest is the same, she'd spit it up after every meal. Hated the sight of it."

I noted, with relief, that he'd signaled for another round. "Pediatrician said not to force it. We buy oat milk now and she's as healthy as can be. Pretty little thing with big brown eyes and white blond hair."

He was leaning forward, watching my face. I sat back, looked away.

(section in yellow in editing process)

I am against yellow hair as a matter of principle, and "white-blond" children always put me in a bad mood. Matthew continued, seemingly unaffected by my silent, sullen hostility.

"And her voice! Perfect pitch. She sings Christmas carols like a little blond angel…" His voice cracked and I looked up to see him staring into his glass.

"As a matter of fact, she's been covered with hair since the day she was born. Baby fine silk, from head to toe. Like a pelt. Like an Easter chick."

My mouth fell open.

"They call it hypertrichosis. Her big sister is normal, but Emma . . . it's a genetic anomaly – something with chromosomes. Specialist says she could still outgrow it. Just turned six. Beautiful little girl, anyway. Smart as a whip."

He looked down, then away, made a noise in his throat. Shook it off, locked eyes with me, lifted his glass. "Hey, you have good taste in whiskey, you know that? Not every day I meet a women who appreciates a fine single malt!"

I lifted my glass in return. Should have said nothing but that is not in me, apparently.

"All babies are kind of hairy, though aren't they?" Trying to be helpful. "But then it falls out, usually, I thought . . ." Lost and rambling. I know less than nothing about babies.

He seemed appreciative, though. Nodding as if to say, thank you for listening but I am not overly concerned. Then he told a joke and I grinned way before he finished. I couldn't hear him through the boom of my own thoughts: It is your measured reasonableness I envy. You really believe life is fair because in the end we all come out even.

"I want to tell you a story," I said this out loud, to him. "It relates, but indirectly."

He nodded and half stood up. Then pulled, with easy strength, my wing chair closer to his, a hand on each fat cordoroy arm. "It's kind of a long story," I warned, and his eyes did not leave my face.

"Few years back I was driving south to see family.

Usually I fly but, it was the outbreak so, had to drive. And I'm not the greatest driver and the further south you go, the faster they drive. Refrigerated trucks barrelled behind my sardine box of a rental, horns blasting. We hit some traffic, think there was an accident, and this weird truck pulled up next to me — it was covered with holes. Like portholes on a ship. Like swiss cheese, only all the holes were evenly spaced and all the same size. I saw these faces in there. Pale faces with light colored eyes – shades of brown and blue. They were pigs.

"One pig looked straight back at me and held my gaze until the driver took off. There was a crushing pain in my chest. My foot was shaking on the accelerator and cars behind me were honking. I thought I was having a stroke or a heart attack. I needed a bathroom and a Xanax and my GPS said the next exit was Dillon, South Carolina.

"Dillon, I learned, is home to a Super-Walmart, a web of chicken plants owned by the same guy – you probably know him – and not much else. But the Xanax helped and pretty soon and I was calm. And brave. Reckless is the word my mother likes to use.

"I sat in the Super-Walmart parking lot and Googled factory farms near me and discovered that the main headquarters was down this little crooked little road with no sign and then to the right. Literally right behind the Walmart. So, you know, I drove up in there. And it looks exactly the way one might imagine: Monster stacks of grey concrete and that old-timey looking electric barbed-wired fence off far back from the road.

"The security at the gate isn't as heavy as one might think. Just two stone-faced heavy-set, dark-skinned locals in black uniforms with radios. They weren't menacing, just humorless and wary.

"I told them I taught theory at the Culinary Academy and was interested in Perdue's proactive take on environmental and animal welfare concerns. About key production innovations involving calming herbs and whole spectrum lighting. If I could speak with someone about arranging a tour — a class visit — we could likely find room in next semester's budget. They got on their radios as I prattled on.

"Cent-com says you best go by the hatchery," they said. "It's just off main road. Circles back around from the Walmart." She handed me a pamphlet, like a souvenir. It read, 'Welcome to Perdue: A Handbook for Plant Visitors.'

"Twenty minutes later a thin, pleasant, washed-out looking Tim, manager of Perdue's largest chicken hatchery in South Carolina, was handing me a pair of hospital-fresh shoe covers, a big white smock and a plastic head gear. Just like that! I couldn't believe my luck. Sometimes, I think, it's what others think of as deficiencies — my aimlessness, general randomness, unlikely or inappropriate dress — that has served me in ways impossible to quantify.

"So Tim, you can picture him right? Tim led me through a maze of corridors while explaining how they "hatch-out" 6,000 baby chicks every three days. "Perdue truly has it down to a science," he said this with genuine reverence. I know he meant it. He led me into a sort of warehouse with a cold, wet cement floor. And then I smelled death. One minute I was encouraging Tim to tell me more. Next moment death vapor penetrated every mucous membrane — nose, mouth, eye sockets.

"You know how in old forensics shows they say corpses have a distinct and unforgettable smell. So this warehouse was either recently filled with a dumpster full of dead bodies or fifty dumpsters of dead chickens. I stifled my reaction and Tim just kept talking — no reaction. He didn't smell it! He went on about giving school kids tours, because they, too, loved to see the baby chicks. We crossed the death room to another door, our destination. It was cement as well but narrow, with stainless steel on both sides.

"To the left was a wall of metal doors — like a business pod hotel. On the right were filing cabinets with shallow drawers. Like steel lingerie drawers, stacked ten or twelve feet high. Tim pulled open a drawer and it was full of yellow balls of fluff. Dazed yellow chicks. I cupped together my hands and he put there a blind-looking baby who curled into my palms, soothed, I believe, by the warmth of a bigger animal. I could grab her and run — but where to? And then what? But Tim plucked her from the nest I'd made with my hands, dropped her back into the drawer and pushed it shut.

"I had to stay in control. Change happens when everyone does their part and getting shot in the back for federal agriculture terrorism would not help that baby. So when he asked if I wanted to see the eggs I stayed upbeat, chattering on about god knows what as he pulled open a steel door — like the kind in a bank. Inside was very warm ith dim red lighting. Rows of identical white eggs on shelves. Tim said that "they'll be hatching soon — they hatch all at once. Timed down to the minute. Perdue really has it down to a science," he added.

"But two baby chicks lay on the cold cement, struggling on the shards of their baby chick shells. They'd hatched early and had fallen off the egg shelf. I willed my face into neutral but my every cell was screaming The babies! Pick up the babies! Seconds ticked by. 'Sometimes one or two might hatch a little early or a bit late,' he said, gestured towards the squirming chicks. He leaned in to grip the lever on the vault-door and I put one hand on my head to keep it from exploding.

"But — um — aren't ya gonna . . . put them on the other side? With the other chicks?

"'Oh sure, I'll take care of it in a minute," he said, closing the heavy door. "They're pretty tough. I'll show you out first.'"

Matthew made a whistling sound through his teeth. "Jeeze." He looked away, shook his head. "So you think he just left them to die, huh? For someone in the business, that's a lot to take in. Wow. Gotta feeling I won't be getting much sleep tonight. It's definitly not supposed to be like that."

I searched his face for sarcasm or artifice of any description, but he seemed genuinely affected. And what more could I ask of a total stranger who earns a living doing the very thing I've learned to fight? We meet in a bar, the winner and the loser. Tired of working and tired of fighting.

I needed to justify what I knew I was going to do. And here's the thing, he wasn't actively pillaging and plundering, at least not that particular Tuesday night. He was just wanting to be liked, get along, get laid, forget his hairy gene pool—just let everything be okay for one evening. That's what most of us want, at least some of the time. Relief washed over and I felt myself smiling.

You know what came next. We went up to his suite.

There was an sack of golf clubs in the bedroom and his wedding band on the sink. A curved corner of glass and the incredible height from downtown. I wanted a bath and he gave me my privacy for as long as it took. When I climbed out there was classical music. I hummed along, drying off. His suitcase was open in the closet facing the powder room, and lying on top was a white shirt, neatly pressed. I put that on. It was big as a dress. Dense soft cotton with a chemical smell. I couldn't remember anything that flat and clean against my skin since my uniform at St. Paul's. And why I would suddenly remember my achingly self-conscious sixth grade self, arranging and rearranging my hair in the basement Girl's Lavatory is anyone's guess.

I played in the mirror, examined the contents of his black skin-leather pouch, splashed on his cologne. All this time he didn't say anything, or try to come in, or rush me at all. However. When I finally emerged he was completely naked. Just standing there naked, eyes closed peacefully. I was confused because, for one thing, I'd assumed that he would take the lead. As for the rest of it, well. His body wasn't ugly or wrong or anything, it was just really very different from anyone I'd ever been physically close to.

But we'd got this far and I had nowhere else I wanted to sleep and it was exciting, I can say that. So it was on me to bring the sexy back. So I fixed it. I closed my eyes and kissed—softly, with dry lips. No response. He just held his position, sober and naked and waiting. A challenge? And more significant than the question, I suppose, was my response. Confused and anxious I pressed up against him. Nothing. I licked his pink nipple and then I bit down. Well, that did it! Game on! A sharp intake of breath as he grabbed both my shoulders, hard. Thrust and held me out at arm's length.

And then on the bed, on the floor, against the enormous plate glass. Gripping my flesh, leaving red marks that would later turn purple. But first there was me spread open in the big chair, the tender skin of my inner thighs finely grated with his stubble and I heard him say "Good god!" And then, "It's so dark!" When he came I imagined his sperm shooting into my vagus nerve and into my brain, sharp and white. I felt that I was receiving his power.

Ms. Cecile Fatiman! Mam'zelle Défilée-la-folle! My head, drunk and irrational, garbling nonsense from HelloCast black history docs and half a semester of Feminist Criticism. Ms. Tsi Czi aka Queen Dowager of Concessions, stupid Tehamana, practical Mary Ellen Pleasant. Ladies! He is our destruction.

We were together the next day and half of the next. He rescheduled his flight. Walking through the little park by the water he said "everything's really working out. I mean, between you and me, I'm like Midas this quarter. Gonna pull the trigger on Jo'burg this year or next. And those jokers down in Palm Springs, they have no idea! And you, well, you're really terrific.Palm Springs . . .and you — well, you're really terrific . . ." I reached up to touch his face, to see if Midas could work in reverse. "Hey!" He blocked my wrist with a boxer's reflex. Grabbed and held it. "You're an interesting kid, you know that?"

Going back to his suite that night we shared an elevator with a yellow-haired teenager in a pea coat. Matthew planted himself in front, pretended to notice a stray eyelash. Traced my bottom lip with his finger. I tasted salt, caught my breath as the girl blinked in fascinated disgust. It was a long ride to the twenty-eighth floor, and I swallowed several times to keep down the acid. I really tried. But when the doors opened I stepped out quickly, brushed against her."Your father is next," I said softly, lips nearly touching her earlobe. The effect was superlative. The doors closed on the stunned girl and the elevator continued its ascent.

On Sunday we played in bed and strolled the city and he bought me stuff to wear. Its not like I'm completely unfamiliar with downtown, but I'd never seen Matthew's downtown. It was a different world: a world of smiles, a world without the tyranny of cool. A world without messy identities and complicated factions. It was sparkling, clean, animated and friendly. We drank wine and ate and fucked and toasted the beginning of him and the end of the me.The old me, the old Charlotte who got laughed at and picked on. Because the world smiled at the new Charlotte, the Charlotte who had Matthew's absolute attention. The world smiled; benevolent, forgiving and generous. And why not. Matthew had money and drive and a clear path, and a wife who worried and made him a home and stayed out the way and also he had immortality, however hirsute, in the shape of his female progeny. I didn't feel bitter, though. I was happy and relieved to finally be inside.

We had dinner in the most beautiful restaurant ever. It was like a museum inside and I felt like a princess. The jealous gay waiter watched closely as I considered, in a moment of insanity, the "humanely raised and finished" coq au vin. I shook it off, though. I haven't had meat for over two years, but I had some sort of craving. South Africans say dyikioilu to describe a hunger only concentrated protein will satisfy — but this wasn't that. Something internal was off: I was happy and at the same time unwell.

I'm ashamed to say that I ordered the bouillabaisse despite the boullion. It was beef boullion. The waiter said it plainly, eyes boring into my skull —but I pretended not to hear and it all went over Matthew's head. Yeah, the lobster and shrimp were cellular, but the salmon was bone-meat and the broth was made with real beef stock. Which seems pretty harmless to the average civilian but not to me because bouillon is made from spent dairy cow, belly and teats enormous from too many forced pregnancies on a 300 head "small family farm" in a place like Vermont being forced onto a truck with a tazer if she balks then they poke it in her anus but she is frozen in fear and cannot move or breath so they drag her down and into the place that smells of fresh blood and the sicky-sweet smell of congealing blood and she cried big red tears fell down her face because when cows cry they cry red tears and they cry before slaughter because they are so very afraid and that not even bone-meat friendly journalists ever get to witness the actual slaughter. Because they cry and they know that unless you are a psychopath you cannot bear to bare witness.

If KJ knew what I was eating we wouldn't even have to have the break up discussion which she has, most likely, already scripted out. Maybe that's part of why I did it. The larger part is less profound though. Bouillabaise is one of those words that looks harder to say than it is and makes you sound sophisticated if correctly pronounced. And without Baton Rouge there would be no Floating French Quarter so believe me when I say I can pronounce it. All that to say, it worked. Matthew's eyes warmed larger and browner as he nodded in appreciation. Returned the menu to the server in a brisk gesture he ordered what I ordered.

"I'll have what she's having," he said. And then, to my delight, he tried to say it, broad mid-western tongue flapping over the delicate syllables like a fish.

The bubbling South African wine he requested was served so cold it was more like dry ice than liquid on my tongue. He told me about the "Mitchell's Plain Collective" that runs the South African vineyard and how their profits help provide food for the pets of poor children. The children come from all over and wait in line with their hungry kittens and puppies. If it weren't for these feeding stations many of them would have to give their pets away. He assumed I would approve, being that I am an "animal lover." Whenever I hear that phrase I think of "nigger lover." Animals have different personalities, just like people. KJ and I are abolitionists and the whole idea of "pets" is problematic. I smiled anyway, because Matthew only told stories he thought would make me smile, laugh or wonder. That level of commitment to my daily happiness was strange and beautiful. KJ usually told me about things she knew would make me rage and fume, and I guess I did the same. Commiseration was our love language.

Sunday morning he rolled over and whispered something into my neck, shaking me free from a dream. I shrieked.

" Wha—it's just me!" he said.

"Sorry! Apologies. I have a... I just—exaggerated startle response!

"Jesus you scared me!" he was smiling, though and I buried my face in the pillow, mumbled about a bad dream. He started stroking my back, the sweet spot on the back of my heart and I melted.

"I feel bad, now. I'm sorry I scared you, Honey."

I've never heard anyone call anyone "Honey" except on old flat-screen 1990's sitcoms and from his mouth it felt like love. The purest kind, and no I don't know exactly what I mean by that but I mean it. He kept his hand there, rubbing.

Then he said, "I just wanted to ask you about the fish, before I forget."

As the back of my heart warmed my chest cavity did too. It warmed and expanded and I heard myself moan.

He laughed.

I cleared my throat a little and managed to say, "what fish?"

"You're really easy to please, ya know that? I really like that about you ...but listen, I gotta ask..."

"Hmmm?"

"The bouillabaisse, it's been weighing on me,"

"Umm. Oh. What?"

He stopped rubbing. "Are we really eating ALL the fish, like every single fish, in the sea?"

I could feel him grinning before I heard him chuckle. He disappeared into the shower and I jumped up and grabbed his skin-leather wallet. Rifled through it without remorse. Colorful foreign money – South African rands would be easy to change. I stuffed a few under into my pillowcase. With cold and rapidly discoloring fingers I pulled out a north American ID and a few credit cards. One card was thicker than the others — one of those corny photoflash things. I held it up to see his wife pop out in 3-d. She looked like hundreds of other women you've seen before. Not like a friend, but also not particularly unlikeable. A bright, practiced expression on her pointy face and something arch in her smile. She was chatting into her right hand, fingers curled around an invisible mike. It was her ring, turned around and cupped the way people do to avoid interference. Next came two plump girls in summer night gowns with matching yellow pageboy haircuts. Singing Happy Birthday to Daaaddy . .

If either child was a gifted singer I wouldn't have guessed it. And they looked normal, over-fed, perhaps, but normal enough. Neither one exceptionally hairy. I wondered why not but lost interest in the question because the shower turned off and I scrambled to put his wallet back together. I wanted to keep pretending, okay? I still do.

Matthew left for the airport in a Lifetime movie-like swirl of urgent calls, cologne and serge and I lingered in the suite, still feeling the pressure on my jaw where he'd held it to kiss. Wrapped up in the robe he'd been using I ordered the most luxurious brunch. Cell-cultured bacon and biscuits with foraged wild blueberry jam and a half-carafe of real orange juice. It looked so pretty when it arrived on its little cart embellished, they told me, with edible flowers grown on the roof. I hadn't much appetite, just wanted to breathe it in and admire it. Poured the orange juice into last night's champagne glass. Stood at the plate glass window and gazed down at Cleveland's petty bourgeoisie. I felt powerful.

Until I had to pee. The urge came suddenly and I almost didn't make it to the toilet, but when I did urine shot out like a fire hose. And the smell was wretched. I stuck my finger in and it tasted like decaying flesh. It rolled over my tongue without dissipating. It clung there no matter how much as I swallowed. And a piece of something, a crunch of grit scraped between my back teeth. And then I was sweaty all of a sudden and sick to my stomach. Head in the toilet but nothing came out, so I let myself drop, Camille-like, to the floor. Relief came from the cold of it and I curled up like a shrimp.

I dipped my index finger in again, coating it. Held it close to my eyeball because I am extraordinarily nearsighted. The upside being that, up close, I can see really, really well. Like microscopes, KJ used to say. Which is useful for blackheads and similarly intimate levels of examination. But what I saw—it makes no sense—yet here it is: tadpoles with metallic tails like arrowheads. Swear to god. Some tails were bent — broken and flapping. It was too much; I closed my eyes. Eyes closed I saw the truth of it — hundreds of thousands of vigorous, white spermbots coursing through my blood vessels, in and out of my digestive organs, searching for eggs.

8.

Will You Please Shut Up Please

A lonely, cynical "Post-Black" senior hopes to set an example for the new girl.

Charlotte Noa Hebert was socially lost and physically awkward. An unlikely object of another girl's singular, bedazzled attention and also an unlikely subject, or actor. How could she possibly have been expected to act? Even without The Crazy. And yet The Crazy was real. The Crazy is how Noa described her range of symptoms and behaviors : the perpetual scraping of skin, the shedding and regenerating of the yellow-gray skin of social awkwardness which — she would proclaim- both characterized and made a caricature out of her childhood and youth.

A love affair. If only! If only she could reconcile the eccentric. And discard the ill-fitting and unbecoming disguises which never disguised anything anyway. If anything, the personality assessments (10 Tells: Do You Lack Confidence?), spontaneous name changes (Hi, I'm Charlotte! Hey, call me Nicole), and also the inexpertly applied formaldehyde flattener does little more than highlight persistent knots and kinks.She'd only wanted to smooth the front edges – the knotty, crispy fringe bristling up and out from both temples – without frying off her hairline. Why can't they just laythefuckdown and blendthefuckin? Baby-hair bangs are supposed to look wispy. Accidental and effortless.

There once was a time, pre-Horaceville, when Noa's after school routine revolved around certain trendy HelloCasters – their practical advice and true-life dramas. She lusted after their Tooth Paint and EmoEyes. She memorized good comebacks and practiced twisting up her mouth in the mirror. Most efforts leading to cruelly predictable results.

Ironically enough, blending in is easier at Horaceville (or Oldschool Academy). Horaceville girls are impervious to fashion, blissfully ignorant of current events, and are, broadly speaking, dismissive of most cultural trends. Be they "urban" or "local" the answer was very likely no.

INSERT Ambassador

CUT OR PUT ELSEWHERE :(Have you already skipped to the end? If so, you already know that Noa has committed a cowardly, even treasonous, act. Worse still, in lieu of apology she has likely attempted to link her actions and inactions to some sort of celestial phenomena. Like Chinese astrology. Noa's birth totem is the Ox, Ox Outside the Gate. A gentle, wistful, domesticated animal, OOG forever hovers near the farmhouse. Nevertheless – and this is key – she will not easily come in to graze.

Onward. Before things got hot, before the exhibition and debasement, before the commencement of an unhappy sequence of events which would, eventually, drive our hero deep into the bowels of craven fear, before all that and for just a few glistening moments, Noa would glow. So let us begin there,)

On the rolling campus of the Horaceville Academy in Maryland, it was a Sunday morning, all covered in dew.

A chilly Sunday morning and Noa, having checked into Breakfast Club in time to sign out Petey, is practically jogging. The giant poodle-labrador-terrier — the Academy's latest addition to its motley pack of registered Comfort Canines — is the embodiment of exuberance and Noa makes small effort to contain him. He pulls her like a sled. Through the rambling old antebellum Big House and past the freshman dorm. Then down the riding hill and by the time they pass the gatehouse he doesn't have to pull.

There they go, two mixed breeds in the white suburban wilds. Healthy and active and full of, well. If not exactly promise then certainly a kind of eventualness. And not a trace of her usual wincing-angsty-cringe because this morning she, Noa, has a date. Sort of. She will have coffee with X — off campus — at that cool indie place on the edge of town. FweePeeps is, technically speaking, within school's jurisdiction, so it's not like they are breaking any rules — Noa, who has a complicated relationship with rules, must remind herself of this.

Infact, what is to come, what they have planned, is perfectly legal and perfectly wholesome (her mother's word). And yet. As Noa and Petey gallop down the bike path Noa worries. She'd given X the impression she was a regular when, in truth, she'd only been to FweePeeps twice. It was the kind of place that blasts electric blues onto the front sidewalk where you can sit on lounge chairs facing a hardware store and Seoul Fud's House of SeiTan. Too far out of the way for Horaceville girls, who have made a weekend tradition of taking over the spacious Fonbooth at Starbucks. Noa and X, surrounded by civilians, will finally be sort of alone.

Noa noticed X straight away because she sparkled. An inadequate description, agreed. Yet that's the most Noa could say, back then, about the physical manifestation — the corporal being — that was X. Years later Noa would remember her as diminutive, puckish. Exquisitely beautiful and weirdly confident. Protruding jaw with an upturned mouth like an elf. Still, if X— a junior year transfer from Baltimore, were not the sort to sparkle, had she failed to sparkle, Noa could hardly be expected to not have noticed the new girl. Horaceville Academy has less than 20 Black students at any one time.

X had a big mouth. Not wide and stretchy like Noa's but coy and puffy. Tucked and puckered like a fat, silky pouch of potpourri. Noa admired her throaty outspokenness. Paired, as it was, with restraint. Noa marvelled at X's ability to maintain a base level of coherence no matter how combative her opinion. Noa did not trust herself and so kept most thoughts glued tightly to her head. Noa was charmed and also intimidated by the sharp little package of directives, lust, expectations and self-possession that was X. Noa, who had once made a serious hobby out of urinating while standing erect and facing the toilet to demonstrate to herself the reversibility of gender conditioning, finds it easier to hold back than to stop midstream.

Yet X would hit it on the head, wouldn't she?

"It's hard," Noa would tell her, by now deeply involved in the narration of a Life-Lesson-Taught-and-Learned, her favorite kind of story to tell, both then and now. "It's hard," Noa repeated, well into her second rice chai, licking the foam. "Jin, for example, is a natural poet. She's still learning English and yet her writing is gorgeous."

X had sucked in her cheeks like a Jet Beauty of the Week, but on X the effect looked natural. She nodded, pupils dilating and retracting like binoculars, as if searching for the right focus for Noa's outline.

"Intro to Comp, right?" X was so thoroughly attentive that Noa embarrassed, glanced away and back.

"Umhum," Noa lifted her cup to examine X without being obvious. An explosion of impossibly thick lion's mane locs framed her narrow, highly symmetrical face. Noa's face was round and flat like a plate.

She continued. "And Susan Waller could give zero fucks about beauty. So Jin — her name is Jin — writes about the sky 'yawning over' her grandmother's village like a 'sweet, faded dream. And Waller marks it up, in red pen – natch. 'Dangling participle. Subject-verb agreement.' I know they're overworked, but good christ!" X was silent as she extracted a large navel orange from her bag and Noa stalled, recalculating. Dial it down, now. Wrap it up.

Noa shrugged and gulped her chai. "It's institutional, though. Not really her fault,"

X nodded, comprehending everything. Dug her nails into an orange to peel it.

Noa might have stopped there, but she could not. She needed X to know that, indignation aside, she does have sympathy for Susan Waller, and for all the plump Mrs. Wallers of the Western world. The well-meaning, uncreative, over-educated self-righteous shepherds of the dark-skinned downtrodden. She is Noa the oldgirl, Noa the Fair-Minded. X will admire her sense of balance.

X is still nodding, sucking and chewing, and Noa, encouraged, throws back her head, rolling and reckless. "She was literally in tears. I'm like, 'Listen, Jin. Susan Waller is no literary genius. She is not the arbiter of literary promise. Your talent is extraordinary. One day you'll write incredible . . .memoirs from Canton, or whatever you want . . .'"

Noa tucks her lips over her front teeth, a tick she'd never quite outgrown. Ever since their annual July 4th when her uncle sang out across the backyard croquet field , "Come-on Lips! It's your turn! Are you playing or not?" Everyone laughed. Noa later found a cocktail napkin on the back veranda. Someone had scribbled of stick figure with two long braids and big eyeglasses. The eyeglasses covered half her face and her grotesquely exaggerated bottom lip took up the rest.

"'But in the meantime,' I told her, 'Just view these

assignments as spelling and grammar games,'"
Now approaching the finale. "A task in a series of
tasks to complete. A means to an end!'" Noa was
beaming, then. Triumphant.

Bits of amber twinkling in her eyes, X swallowed
what remained of her orange. Her eyes were on
Noa's mouth.

Watching X's throat ripple made Noa think of the
translucent green lizards down south. Attracted to
people's windows at night, if the light is shining the
right way, you can watch the insects they consume
move through their necks and stomachs.

"But couldn't you . . .couldn't she combine the
two?" A perfectly reasonable question. "Can't you
maybe help her figure out how to build on her
beauty of expression, and also, like, work on
grammar and sentence structure at the same time?"

A question that so shocked and deflated Noa that
she went on a rambling defensive, and this, sadly,
is characteristic of Noa. Although Noa lives in a
state of perpetual en guarde she is unprepared for
this sneak attack. This friendly fire. Noa is unused
to being heard with such aggressive clarity and now
lay supine on the cement floor, arms and legs
wiggling. Noa would not let this show. She laughed
and deflected and minimized and diminished and
even as she rambled it did not occur to her to say the
one thing Noa knows to be true:For Jin, Noa and X

there can be no combining. No synthesis. Coloured people have to make choices, and really, X didn't know anything—she was only a junior.

This thought sticks and fleshes out. Takes shape and replicates: X is a sixteen-year-old junior transfer with limited life experience. X was very likely recruited by SteamSTARS as part of the Academy's frantic effort to raise Horaceville's testing averages by luring as many hyper-achievers from local charter schools. You are quick and bright , Ms Thang, but you are naive!

Noa, feeling better, sits back and watches X's pretty face, soaking her in with fresh eyes.

You were raised by a set of grass-rootsy-crunchy Black parents, both of whom, are, to this day, obsessed with your cognitive and emotional growth. They work "meaningful" jobs in the "Black community." The neighbor lady librarian spoon-fed you and your friends Black history after school and your grandparents took you to church.

X was still sucking on her orange slice. Eyes on Noa's face, her gaze soft. Dreamy.

Noa sits up straight. An electric jolt, a happy realization! Easing back in the chair, the little muscles around her eye sockets and jaw uncurl. And there in lies your weakness, my dear. You are a precious, fragile black orchid. You lack experience.

You've not been naked and terrified and inspected and examined under the glare of ugly white light.

insert here ambassador 2

This year, like all three years before, Noa fulfills her graduation service requirement with STEAMstars — that's what they are meant to call the Writing Lab now. Noa, who has never aspired for "star"dom in any subject with a math component, finds the new name obscenely misleading. An assertive group of alumnae—a WASPy clique of bored moms—on a mission to keep the crumbling old school from falling too far behind the times. Thanks to their efforts, Horaceville's once-modest community tutoring initiative has become a lushly funded model for what "independent" schools can contribute to "local communities." This year saw a cash infusion leading to thirty new Macs, a 4-D language lab. And the same dozen or so peer tutors like Noa — female, introverted, scholarship types with sharp elbows. All nudging one another out the gate in a race towards the fuzzy sort of degree offered at a certain type of college where, Noa often predicts, they will each continue their achingly slow climb up The Golden Rope to the white light of nowhere in particular.

In her reoccurring dream it's a hefty rope made of slippery-smooth fibers. The same kind of rope used to foster trust at Horaceville's semi-annual autumnal "Learning the Ropes" zip-line event. Except that you can't see who, if anyone, is holding the rope or how it's secured. It's just suspended from some point in the sky, and if you don't hold on you fall and die in molasses swamp.

This type of thinking primes the pump and she is showering in fear. Fear diluted in motor oil sprays from the shower head, clinging and black and thick.

Noa understands that most people in her class will never have to worry about a career or anything near the base of Maslow's Pyramid. Which is their good luck (she has often reflected), for what possible position, what job function could a Master of English perform that a Bachelor of English could not? This is a good question for the Black, well-bred husband who is a person just like you so now, the two of you up further still, to a doctorate for at least one of you. Dr and Mrs. Puttbutt.

There must be an end to the rope. Noa, who is profoundly nearsighted (which means, metaphysically, fear of the future), must believe in the existence of some sort of a waystation. A platform that makes sense and feels good. Having rejected organized religion by the age of ten, she has only her Black American middle-class faith in congeniality, caution and diplomas. And in the meantime, there must be value in helping "disadvantaged youth" pass Waller's English Composition. Noa's mother is proud of her, though. Proud enough. Noa squeezes shut her eyes.

Insert here ambassador

It was Monday it was Tuesday. Day 1, week five of the AP English research lab elective and Noa is stewing in rage-juice. Struggling to make sense of the shocking grade scrawled on the last page of her first major assignment. Master of English Carol Leong had concluded that Noa's ethnographic essay was worth exactly eighty-two points out of one hundred. She'd offered, by way of explanation, a paragraph of insights and suggestions, lightly penciled in girly, rounded cursive which made her think of a quote: in the neat handwriting of the illiterate— Noa's upper lip had curled up and she willed it to flatten. Whoever said that was genius—shut up, Noa! Grow the fuck up.

She tried to focus on Leong's critique, but a bloody film — a sort of translucent membrane — slid first over her left eyeball and then over her right. Giving up, she tucked away her bruised, defiled essay and wills her face into an expression of alert objectivity. Strains to hear through the buzz of white noise.

Failure, so she starts a list: White Noise. Tar Baby. War and Peace. Titles of books so far unread. Noa wills her expression neutral.

A hand shoots up. It is the splayed palm of Oldschool's only male student – Matthew Raymond Carver. His real last name was Pritchard-Carter but Noa had decided that—much like her least favorite writer—Matthew was luxuriating in unearned privilege.

When something called the "Oldschool Community" (a clutch of wealthy Oldgirls and influential faculty) voted to "diversify" the student body by "selectively" admit male students, Noa's mom said they wanted to increase the number of prospective students who could pay full tuition. What they got was Matthew—the well-spoken, attractive and dirt-poor progeny of Maryland's eastern shore. They had to give him a full ride. It was worth it, though. Since his photos started appearing on the school website, catalog had increased

thou Just having his photos judging by how everyone treats him, just being Matthew was enough. Mister I'm just a white guy doing my best to make life good in my world which is white and it ain't fancy and damn it that's okay.

Matt, one of Leong's WASP-y favorites, has a question "for the room."

"It's about anonymity and research protocol." Clearing his throat. "Say you have permission from your source, your informant, whatever you call it given your discipline," he seems genuinely nervous and Noa wills herself to not hate him. But you can't, can you? You can't because you are a hater of people.

Master of English Carol Leong bobs her head and makes an encouraging noise. Leans against her desk to give him the floor while Noa strains to hear above the howling through her ears. "I'm Matt, by the way," this with an insouciant little wave.

Scanning the room he continues. "Say you might want to publish, but you start to sense that she . . . the informant . . . doesn't quite realize what she signed up for? In terms of privacy."

Noa's heart was pounding, working hard for no reason. She couldn't recall drinking any water that morning so maybe her blood had thickened. Dehydration.

"Okay, I'm not explaining this well. So, yeah! Starting again. I did my ethnography at the East Baltimore SNAP assistance center," Noa put an index finger to her lip and found it cracked and peeled. Dessicated. She licked the wound and tasted blood. An early warning sign for a stroke? Noa is digging through her bag for a loose baby aspirin.

"Could you be more specific, Matt?" This from Leong, whose tone, it seemed to Noa, had gone from fawning to something tighter. A cover up! I see you, Carol Leong. You love Matt so damn much. You are, I'm fairly sure, engaged to an older version of Matt. I'd put money on it.

With every drop of saliva she could siphon Noa swallowed, but the bile bubbled back up. She could taste it. Happy climbing, girl friend. I wish you double-happiness, Sister Carol. May your relative whiteness be forever on the increase.

Matt shuffles papers, fumbling. Stalling?

Leong offered encouragement. "I thought you did a nice job with this assignment? Okay gang, let's help him out. This is a seminar and additional input would be helpful? There is so much talent in this room, you guys."

Run for the toilet. Noa considered this option while other students—mirroring their instructor— posed to Matt only the most equivocal questions. Which led to Matt saying he'd like to share some of the audio "ifnobody minds, of course. Don't want to take up all the time— "

Then came a disembodied female voice— a soliloquy in screeching ghettoise! ". . . need my check to-day! Bae back there acting like she stupid. Now. You tell me. You-tell-me why it matter, though?"

Noa noted, with disconnected interest, that she could both hear and smell her own breath. Synesthesia! She considered that phenomenon while her left hemisphere processed and categorized incoming data. What is the phrase . . . Performative! Matt's source was performing female victimization. Now Noa could see everything, all of them and all of it, all at once and in a flash. Welfare Lady was performing for Matt. Surely she knew he was recording. Why on eart—

"You know 'cause . . .he all up in my face and Immatypeofperson who—"

Noa was certain she detected amusement behind the whine. Was Welfare Lady having fun? Noa's breath-fumes, having gathered strength, were now so thick and caustic she could feel her tooth enamel dissolve. Sticky tongue, crackled lips. Self-immolation is a thing that happens and I could spontaneously combust.

A burst of giggle escapes the circle of desks. Noa, shifting her weight, nearly slips off the hard little seat. Who the fuck is giggling?

Now she is sweating. Shut up, Noa and calm the fuck down. This is not your fight not your issue not your monkey not your circus! Matthew Raymond Carter and Carol Leong and Welfare Lady are individual humans on this planet. This thing, whatever it is, is in no way relevant to your climb. They are whomever they are and you are Noa, High Priestess of Chik'n Pepper Curry! Noa, lover of electrical storms! Noa, 780 verbal high scorer! You are not burning, you are not drowning. Please. Now Noa is begging. Contemporaneous Noa is on her knees pleading with Very-Near Future Noa. Only eight more minutes to go. Please just act like everyone else.

"Seriously?" An outburst followed an impatient noise — like spray escaping a helium balloon. It was the giggling girl.

It was X!

Noa turned her head stiffly back to center, right side of her face burning.

"How do you mean?" This from Matt, who had paused the audio as Noa stared deeply into the lines of her oak laminate desk.

Look up! Noa willed herself. Look at him because he is speaking! Everyone is looking at him but you.

"I'm sorry but this is crazy. You can't just—"

"Are you offended? Because this is an ethnography. In no way did I—"

Matt raised his hands, exposing both palms in a helpless gesture. He scanned the room, eyes resting briefly on Noa, who was instantly distracted by the unusually pale blue tint of his irises. How had she never noticed this before? They were nearly free of color. Color-free! Matt, frowning, looked away.

Next she wondered why she found it such a challenge to act normal, to be and act natural in any sense of the word, why she had to control her every action as though she were two heads on one torso. Like that movie where a big pimple sprouts up and starts talking to people—Shut up shut up shut up.

Leong scanned the room with bureaucratic evenness: "If anyone finds this research topic or Matt's . . .methodology in any way offensive, we should take a moment to discuss those feeli— "

X interrupted. "I'm sorry, but no. It is offensive. It should be offensive to everyone. But he's the one who needs to discuss his—not feelings. His motives. His motivation— "

"Am I missing somethi-"

X stepped square into his annoyance.

"I mean, Matt —   that's your name, right?

Something made you hesitant to share, a little nervous. Ask yourself why?"

"Obviously I was nervous because I was the first one to s— "

"Try harder!"

"Listen I have not a c—"

"You want validation because you have guilt. Ask yourself why." X had a voice that carried without rising in pitch or volume. And though leaning forward, her interest in his response seemed pure. Academic.

Matt stared, jaw tight like a trap. X, chin resting on one hand, met his eyes with the unhappy smile one might give to a stranger's exhausting toddler.

Matt gave in. "Honestly I'm pretty sure you're about to tell m—"

"You liked it, am I wrong? You like being the only smart white dude in a hood full of poors. And you knew you'd get good audio because whatever our circumstances, Black people are good storytellers."

"You do not know me, okay? I am no—"

"And I'm not sayi—"

"Exactly what is it you're sa— "

"Exploitation. That's what you did. That's what just happened."

Radio silence.

"A powerful reaction and absolutely valid," Leong, having regrouped, stood behind her desk now, authority restored. She beamed at X for a beat or two longer than necessary but X didn't notice. She was scribbling something in her notebook. "And I want to take a minute to applaud you, Stephanie X, for having the strength to articulate something I suspect was on the minds of many of us." Now everyone was smiling at X. Everyone but Matt, who was putting away his equipment.

Leong glanced at Noa for the briefest of seconds; found their way back to to Matt.

"And Matt. While some of that was probably tough to hear, and I have to say I don't necessarily agree with everything 100 percent, you can read my comments on the last page.I'll bet you can think of ways to rework this project – I can help if you'd like – make your true intentions align better with your presentation."

Noa's mouth was hanging open so she willed her jaw shut.

Said Leong, "So thank you, everyone! That's a lot to unpack, for all of us . . ."

Noa met Leong's eyes and they both looked away, fast. Noa imagined everyone looking at her, waiting for her, silent and expecting and she wished that they would not. Why didn't any of the other coloreds speak up? There were several others, sort of. A sulky-ebonics-slinging Latinx. And that bewildered-looking Hong Kong girl—bossy and staccato enough before the meeting wasn't she? On and on about the herb tea in the black tea tin but not a squeak from her now. Shut up Noa! No one is looking at you! But when she glanced up to sneak a look at the clock she found herself being studied, by the probing, gentle, thoughtful gaze of pretty little X. Now both of Noa's cheeks burned.

"Okay. We can talk about this more next week, but for now look at the syllabus . . .okay really quick. Someone read at the top of page two for next week?"

Sexy-Sulky took over while Noa wondered if there was a word for being humiliated and pleasured simultaneously. Probably in German. X! What the fuck are you. How are you so clear and clever and confident? While Noa just wobbles. Exhaustively questioning reality and her perception thereof. Noa could only take a stand when no stand was necessary. Last fall, for example, when it was a question of whether or not the beneficiaries of STEAMstars should be invited along to the staff picnic, Noa had been passionate and unbending in her insistence that the staff picnic was so-called because it was for staff. When there was nothing to be defended Noa was a fearless warrior.

When class ends Noa has a plan — a sensible and irreproachable course of action. She folds her brow into a preoccupied expression. She would sprint to the library to check the evening STEAMstars drop-in list. She had just turned the corner when she nearly collided with X, who was grinning as she sidestepped, dramatically, out of the way. Disorientated, Noa slammed the left side of her body, wrist, hip and hand, hard into the cold metal doorpost.

XXX (insert part 4 as yet unwritten The Ambassador's blue Cadillac is flattened by a refrigerated truck in the Delmarva factory farm region enroute to Horaceville)

It was Wednesday it was Thursday. Thursday evening and Noa and Jin were finishing up. Gathering printouts as Jin put on her childish pink windbreaker, swinging her shiny ponytail from underneath the neck of it. Noa, whose equally childish French braids were frizzy and delicate, had, from age ten, never stopped wondering what it might be like to have durable, glossy hair with staying power, hair that flapped in the wind like a kite, always to fall right back, never losing its center.

Jin scurried off to catch her bus as Noa headed toward the office, sorting through messy worksheets, wondering what could be tossed and what should be neatly filed away, never to be retrieved. It may be worth noting that although she cannot help but dwell endlessly on the far-away past, Noa is unusually stubborn in her refusal to acknowledge the immediate past.

Zipping around the corner for the second time that week she narrowly missed a collision with her noisy new colleague. Noa caught herself this time, recovered and straightened, but before she could force a smile and say, "Have a good weekend!" or "Headed home?"—things you are supposed to merrily shout to people you barely know —X blurted, "Want to see that doc at the playhouse this weekend? It's a special showing of . . ."

The rest of the invitation was buzzing static for Noa. Noa, who wasn't stupid — who would coyly confess her verbal (never math) SAT to anyone if anyone would ever ask (no one ever did) — wasn't the quickest thinker either. LGBTQ X=lesbian. Then came a second realization, far more shocking: X = Asking Me Out.

Had Noa been granted the powers of invisibility for which she'd spent her elementary school years praying, she could have raised one stiffened arm, fingers outstretched and in one sweeping arc frozen time to the millisecond. She would have stilled the growth of the spider plants, the twinkling obsidian in X's brown eyes. And had Noa been Hamlet or maybe Orlando she could have turned and described the feeling as a chin-deep submersion in clean black water. A shared salt lick. Starlight.

Noa is just Noa, though, her reply overdue. Overwhelmed and flattered and stunned, she did what came naturally. She acted as though she were not. She pretended that X's invitation had been anticipated, and that if X hadn't finally come out with it she would have been forced to ask her out herself, just to keep things moving along. Worries and fears circling her head like cartoon bats, Noa smiles blandly, avoiding X's eyes. She smiles into X's narrow forehead. Scribbling down phone numbers, there is a short memory lapse (8-3-2? 3-2-8?); but this is unremarkable. She covers it up. And then, in the low register voice she always uses unless she forgets to, Noa says, "Sunday then," so cool and natural and seductive, as if she was accustomed to making dates with people.

That night Noa is warm and light-headed. But in the morning she is icy cold. Her face feels greasy, hair plastered up on one side like carpet. Noa would have to back out. She would tell X first thing. It would be easy because she would just tell her the truth. But actually it didn't even occur to her to tell the truth, because if she were to tell the truth she would have to say, "X! I'm afraid of you! I'm afraid of your perception, of your intelligence that is not buried in garbage and pathologies! I'm flattered but I know I will disappoint you!" In the end it didn't matter though, because X didn't tutor on Fridays. Noa had forgotten.

Friday night in a Fonbooth, throat twisting with anxiety, Noa is calling X. She'd misplaced the number but had pulled up the staff roster. Noa dials the seven numbers. Busy. Redial. The lyrical series of beeps is soothing. It's still busy and Noa, compulsive, pushed redial again. Busy still, but now a lurch in Noa's gut. She presses the hang up button on the receiver and dials her own number. The beep sequence matches and Noa, shrieking, slams down the receiver, startling Petey who commences to bark. Noa takes a slow breath. Dials the correct number, X's number.

"Hello?" Picked up on the first ring. Noa isn't ready. She swallows, tries to respond. This triggers wild snorting and coughing and Noa holds the receiver away from her head. Gain control, please.

"Who is this?" Annoyed. Noa panics, wonders if X hadn't been on the other line with someone more together.

"Hi—excu—Noa, Sorry, this is Noa!" she manages, just barely.

"Oh. Sorry! I didn't recognize the number." X's voice didn't soften and Noa tensed. She knows I'm going to flake. Noa imagined herself a beige-colored rat with rotted teeth, backed into the corner of an alley.

"I'm in the Fonbooth," she said. Warmed up her voice, forced it low, low and even. "X, when you asked me to the film I was so surprised and flattered—I agreed when I shouldn't have."

X did not respond. Was she still there? Noa willed herself to not be afraid of silence. But Noa is weak. Where there are gaps, Noa has a caulk gun. "Actually (be silent!)—actually I'm involved with someone (lie!)—long distance (lying cunt!)—a guy."

Noa is exhausted. Deceit. Why is it necessary to complicate everything?

More silence. Noa wonders if X is giggling. Noa wonders if she had not been mistaken in thinking she'd been asked out on a date to begin with. Why is she a miserable egotist? X just wants to make friends at her new job, thought it would be a good film, thought Noa seemed lonely. Noa ducks and covers.

"I mean—if it makes any difference. I mean, if it doesn't—" Noa scrambles backwards, forgetting to modulate her voice.

"Of course it makes a difference," blurts a hot rush of air. Noa's throat itches and she swallows hard to relieve it, but there is no saliva left. She wants to shove her entire hand down her throat to claw at the insides. She is dirty and itchy all over—her scalp and her crotch and her face. Dirty in the light of X's clarity beaming through the phone. Where Noa squeezes shut her pink-rimmed eyes, X charges forward. "It makes a huge difference." X enunciates carefully, as if speaking to a hard-headed child. "I am asking you to a film with me!"

It is Saturday it is Sunday. It will be coffee—less intimate than a film, and more appropriate, in light of Noa's exotic new love life. Noa wakes up early and dresses ridiculously, two braids crossed over her head Laura Ingalls Wilder style; beige sweatpants and army boots. She checks into Breakfast Club and goes to pick up Petey.

Two hours later she sits carefully at the table X has picked and squirms when X says "Nothing for me. I brought an orange!" Noa doesn't feel comfortable sitting in cafes or bars without ordering immediately. Noa carries an unreasonable childhood fear of people thinking she doesn't have any money, that Black people don't have any money. Always expecting something for nothing. Petey, having gobbled down a chunk of biscotti, now sits up to watch the X and Noa with hot-breathed, open-mouthed anticipation.

XXX

It was Monday it was Tuesday. It was Tuesday night and they were on the deck of the Metrodome. Noa didn't want her drink; there was enough fruit in it to make a salad and the ice against her teeth sent electric shocks into her skull. X drank tap water. The club was packed, and everywhere was guys. It might have been Texas night because they were all really big guys. Noa, who is shorter and also smaller than she imagines herself, felt like a little kid at a grownup's party. It was exciting. Noa prayed for cool as she clicked her tongue to the lyrics popping through the bass.

((((We dont own a goddamn thing!

We aint got nothing left!)))))

They squatted on an upstairs catwalk, away from the disco. They ducked under the guardrail and sat perched like pigeons. There was a view of the empty street if they looked straight ahead, and when that became awkward they had only to glance behind for the reassurance of Wranglers and chap-covered legs. One dancer didn't get the memo about the dress code. Impossibly thin with blue-black skin and a face as smooth and open as a child star's, they twisted their neck and shoulders into a loop; curled back out. Slender arms unwinding the rest, white glowing tooth and fingernail paint glowing like phosphorescence.

"What do you want from me, X?" Corny and dramatic. X brightened, as though pleased with Noa's clumsiness. Noa put her glass down, made a mental note to keep her leg still so as not to knock it over.

"You ask me out, I tell you I'm spoken for . . ." Noa took a breath. "I then proceed to expose myself —my watery character—over coffee. I then agree to meet you again, at a gay theme bar, I'm not sure why—"

"I want you to hold me by the back of the neck and kiss me with your whole tongue. I want my wrists to hurt when you pin them over my head in the men's room downstairs. I want to take you to the rose garden by the lake—" (a piece of ice, having slipped from Noa's bottom lip, was now slithering its way down the front of her shirt) "and show you my favorites."

"Really?" Noa stalled as her producer foundered, flipping through upside down and water smudged pages of script. There were options. From the frigid, "But why on earth would I want to participate in any of those activities?" to the slithering and more likely, "But I thought we'd agreed to just be friends?" But typical of Noa, Noa said nothing. Typical because Noa is cowardly.

"I'm sorry," Noa stood. "I have to pee. It's not—"

"One dance!"

"I don't lik—"

"Please!"

"No!"

Noa has a morbid fear of dancing.

"Let me dance for you, then. One song, and then you can run away. Okay? Please?" With X's eyes closed Noa could stare. She studied her face and throat and her thick coils of hair. The disco lights seemed to shelter in otherwise impenetrable swirls and loops, blinking there like stars. Noa looked away to see who was watching; wondered why her face was sweaty and stinging. She wondered if it wasn't time to go back. X was moving around Noa in a circle, brushing closer and closer each time she came around.

"Reminds me of Haiti. I have cousins in Haiti. In a past life they must have danced like this . . ."

X swept her head around, exposing her throat to Noa, then sweeping her head around blocking everything. Noa, swallowing, tried to bounce around so that she wouldn't look too stupid. Giving up she allowed herself to be an audience to X, who was moving her little feet so quickly. When had she taken off her shoes? X was dancing close enough that Noa could smell her, and Noa imagined herself a Hindu prince in a fabulous tent, high on opium and dried figs. Closed her eyes to keep from dizziness.

When she opened them there were only cowboys there and she panicked. Exposed—she'd been exposed and abandoned, but before she could digest this new horror there was X's body, pressing in. Noa didn't move, but there was a gush of relief and she forgot the cowboys, and when X moved in front again, Noa grabbed and held tight her shoulders, wondered at their smallness. X's filthy bare feet kept moving but Noa held her firmly in one place. She felt she could feel the blood cells and the molecules and even the electrons moving through her shoulders. Noa felt greedy.

She ran her hands over X's bare throat, over her big mouth, covering its warmth for a moment. Then both hands in X's scalp, fingers digging in. Noa was a surprise to herself. X's coils responded to the intrusion with a charm defensive. They clung and curled around Noas fingertips. X lifted her own arms up, high like a sati, eyes closed. Abandon! X was giving herself to Noa. Noa, although somewhat familiar with that general impulse, had never before been on the powerful end.

Noa felt X's ribs through her tee shirt: Her stomach, her flat breasts. She imagined she was patting for weapons. Down further still, to her round butt and thick, strong thighs. Her fingers lingered long enough to learn that X was really quite hairy! Noa had not predicted that and she wanted to know more but when her fingers felt the edge of X's underwear, surprisingly slippery and possibly purple, or they could have been chocolate colored, Noa froze. She was suddenly herself again, her outside visible self, and X would certainly betray her. X was really just a stranger, a strange female stranger and Noa was a coward. A coward and a quitter and she had never felt stranger and it was a rush of cold air blowing in at her neck when she pulled away and tore from the Hippodrome onto empty Charles Street.[1]

1. A sticky, bitter taste spreads over Noa's tongue and she fails to scrape her teeth over it without being obvious. The taste increases and her bottom teeth burn because it is acid coming up.

9.

Control Your Face

A lifestyle influencer is forced to witness an obscenity. In real time, in front of her live HelloCast audience.

We. Are. Back! To those of you just joining us, welcome! Welcome to Gracious Living with Nicole Thibidaux! How was that for everyone? Were you able to quiet the chatter? Could you rise above the noisy day-to-day and observe your thoughts as a spectator, rather than a participant? Did you remember to breathe? Excellent. That's super!

"Now. I would like to talk — for just a moment — about this gorgeous Riesling. Now, I know what you're thinking. You're thinking, Riesling? Isn't that for dessert? Not this one! Produced by the House of Mandela in South Africa's Western Cape, quite dry with sharp tannins. Can you smell it? You should be able to smell it now. Isn't that fragrant? That's how you know it's from riesling grapes. Just breathe that in."

"Philadelphia   luvz   u!"   "Smells   just   like honeysuckle!"

"we ♥ you, Nicole!"

"And I love you! All of you! And I adore this wine! Don't you? It pairs with just about anything. But when the weather is this warm I wouldn't think of heating up the kitchen."

"Sending you LOVE and GodBless from South Carolina!"

"So I say, go get yourself a plate and pile it up with grapes, a cake of brie, crackers, a dish of nuts and call it a lunch!"

Nicole, now seated on a stool before a little round table, has before her a charcuterie board. She selects a cracker with cheese.

"There was always something a little steamy. A bit

decadent about grapes. Think of the overripe fruit in an old Dutch still life. Oh my, that's really very good.

"I love CHEESE x2!" "my motto=any kind of cheese goes w anykind wine"

"Milk is for baby cows Nicole!"

"Yes, I am aware of the issues and this is the right time to address some of them. Cheese making is a tradition going back centuries, since before the time of factory farms. And I don't think any of us here would ever want to argue on behalf of the mega dairies of America's far too recent past."

"That's all they got in Chy-nah!""U R my role model!"

"Coloured Zimbabwe salutes you!"

"Yes, you are right. They do still have them in Eastern Europe and in some of the states in the, um, yes the China-Africa agriculture trade zone. They do such terrible damage to our environment, don't they? They really contaminate our air and water. And do you know how much water it takes to raise and feed the average dairy cow? It really is a lot, folks."

Producers roll live feed from the green rolling hills of Vermont. Cows grazing peacefully. Zoom in on the milking barn into what is clearly a wholesome family farm operation.

I think we have all come to understand that factory farming, in general, is simply not sustainable. For that very reason we at Gracious Living support America's small farmers.

Three blond teenage boys, siblings, appear in and out of camera range. They are unhappily doing some sort of barn chore with buckets. They make ugly faces for the camera.

"But for those of us in the States, I am happy to confirm that megadairies are on their way out. And I'm even happier to confirm that the small, family-run dairies of the 1950's are back in business!

Better for our environment, better for our health and some say ... they can taste the difference!"

She takes a bite and says, "Delicious!"

"Now this, this is a very nice substitute for Brie. My interns found this one for today's show and I have to say it is really not bad! In fact it is very, very, nice!"

"Aw come on Mx Nicole u kno its nasty!" "stop lyin girl!"

"No, I mean it! This one is different, it's actually made from cellular technology. However, as of yet, I have to say there is no mass-produced substitute for my two soft-blue favorites. Not one that I could recommend. Not in good conscience, anyway."

"Milk is Murder!!!!"

"Okay, now settle down! My feeling is this: One

does not have to go to such polarizing . . . extremes. Rarely can important issues —and the production of food is certainly an important issue —seldom can they be reduced to right or wrong, black and white. I think this is true, in general principle."

The boys surround one cow. One lifts her tail and exposes her vulva. They are clearly doing this for the camera. He spits on his hand and then rubs his fingers slowly, revoltingly around the rim of the cow's vagina. Another boy uses an object to penetrate the cow over and over again. There is no volume. Nicole continues, unaware.

"But also, when it comes to a food product as culturally significant as these special cheeses . . . think of the concept of terroir in French wine ... we have a shared heritage. A history of survival, of discovery, of pride in an ancient tradition of craftmanship ... let's not be so quick to throw it away, what do ya say?"

But Nicole is receiving a message from the studio through her earpiece. Her face turns rigid as the boys continue to molest and penetrate the cow.

Fradine, frozen before Nicole's hologram, jerks forward to vomit as the live feed goes white and the sound goes to static.

10.

Gracious Living

The Old Black Ones have yet to authorize the release of data collected from the Flesh Tributary Initiative for Improved Eurindigenous Relations. Fradine and Luc wonder over the ethics.

Big Luc says sensibly, "We can see it is working and if we are wise we will let nature take its course and leave well-enough alone—"

"Oh good god!" Fradine returns her tiny cup to its saucer. "The evidence is overwhelming!"

"Anecdotal. We haven't seen the actual data."

Fradine says, "Now you are being difficult on purpose. It's impossible to have a proper discussion when you fold up like this. Think of all the suffering!"

Big Luc expels a puff of air. "En ce moment, right now you sound like your American lady-crush. But exact!"

Fradine checks her smartwatch and says archly, "What is this? Is Luci jealous? It's about time!"

Big Luc picks up her Glowbook and, staring into the screen, says, "If you want to persuade me, use logic—not pathos."

Fradine tries again, "The Caribbean world is sitting on a solution, temporary, of course, but it buys time. The world should know! Think of it like this—we have found a radical treatment for a deadly virus. Not a vaccine, but a treatment to mitigate the toxic effects, however temporarily. It's a breakthrough! To give psychological relief to all those affected. How can we sit and watch others suffer? Are we not then complicit?"

Big Luc says, "Here we must disagree. The flesh tribute system works because it is nebulous. The moment you start collecting your data, putting codes into writing, that is when the whole thing becomes vulnerable. That is what the Old Black Ones know."

Fradine sighs and says,"I may never thoroughly understand the Obos' love for subterfuge. It's not simple mistrust, trust me it is political. They must have their plausible deniability and I find it all very cynical."

Big Luc says nothing and Fradine leans across the table. "Or maybe this is something else — remnants of Euri-colonial shame? I beg you, love of my heart. Come into the light!"

"Ridiculous," Big Luc pushes wire-rimmed eyeglasses back up her broad long nose. "How I feel makes no difference. Why not scribble up a proposal for the Obos? Use your pull and let your voice be heard, woman!"

Sitting up straight, Fradine dabs the corner of her mouth. "I intend to," she says. "That is my intent."

"But, please, in all seriousness. The summit was a lost opportunity for the Diaspora. Think of the chaos in the deep southern states. Would life not be just a little bit better for the majority of its citizens if colored leadership had access to this, how to say, pressure release valve?"

"The Caribbean flesh tribute is just an experiment. One could hardly even call it a system. Ideas are free so why speak as though Caricom is intentionally withholding—"

"Mais ouais, c'est exact! Knowledge is power! Crime has dropped, mushroom and herb growers are happy, people who work in tourism are happy as are the foreign students. Science, even social science, is meant not for your ivory tower! It is for the peop—"

Big Luc finished her wife's sentence.

"Science for the people, ouais ouais ouais. But I am confused, my sweet. Was it not just yesterday when you called me the idealist? In this moment, which one of us is being unrealistic?"

Fradine fell silent.

Then she smiled and said, "Once again we've managed to run off the road. My fault, this time. this much I admit."

Big Luc said, "I'm afraid I've quite lost track, Chou-Chou."

Fradine said patiently, "Her message. Nicole's message to the world, to the diaspora, to all of us—"

Big Luc said, "Ouais, tell me again, what wisdom does the oracular American HelloCaster have to share?"

"Now you are insincere, but I can accept a little ridicule. I think she knows all about our flesh tributes. Moreover, I think she approves. She can't come out and say so, of course, but if you listen carefully she drops all kinds of hints."

Big Luc considers. Improbable, certainly, but far from an impossibility.

"Just think about it! You know the chant, the American protest chant says, 'no justice, no peace.' It is very famous. You hear it in movies and in the news," she adds.

Big Luc was impatient. She really knows how to draw out a thing. "Yes, and what about it?"

"Nicole Thibidaux is a worldly, well-educated woman. What's more, she has Haitian DNA! I suspect she has kept a close eye on us for decades. She understands the power of the flesh tribute. She has been briefed on its effect on our way of living, our Caricom communities. That is the point of her show! It is always possible to lead a gracious life, no matter what. As long as there is a mutual understanding. Notice that I did not say respect. Historically speaking, respect has always been been very difficult for the Eurindigenous...but think about it. Obviously it is impossible to lead a gracious life without 1. Reparative justice and 2. A reliable system of accountability for ongoing offenses!"

Luc's spectacles were sliding down her nose but she didn't push them up. Regarded Fradine for a thoughtful moment. Then pointed up, to the place where the sun would glare were it not for the solar sponge and said, "Are you not losing your time of self-care with your guru? Nicole la formidable? C'est venu, n'est-ce pas?

"Bloody fuck!" Fradine lept from her chair. Jerked open the double doors, slid through the kitchen and down the hall in her Smartsox. Slip-sliding on waxed floorboards, she slapped one palm to the wall, regained her footing. Turning into the windowless, furniture-free media room, she clapped twice. HelloCasting discs mounted above projected a brilliant holographic planet earth into the room's center. The blue-gray walls appeared to balloon and vanish, an illusion created with filters over the lights.

The planet spun on its axis, gaining momentum, and as it whirled it morphed into the elongated shape of a not-quite-human eye. It was the Global Broadcasting Cooperative's logo. The top and bottom lid stretch open impossibly wide, then narrow, meeting in the center like a lizard's eye. The Big View it was called.

Fradine stepped onto the elevated track. EarthTurf clawed at the soles of her Smartsox and Fradine was ready.

♭ ♯ ♭ Welcome to our Gracious Life

 Beauty and discretion

protecting inner counsel,

with outward pre—sent—aaation ~ ♭ ♯ ♭

Fradine willed her brow to unfurl, her jaw to unclench. Now clapped again, and the track begins its rotation, slowly at first, then faster to match her pace. Summers were different when she was small. Always a breeze off the Jacmel Bay. The sun did beat down, but there was no reason to fear it.

The Big View, having disassembled, was now replaced by the whimsical introduction to Gracious Living with Nicole. Optimistic acapella Afra-Pop vocals and Fradine, brightening, lengthens her strides. In the place of the eye was an obsidian-colored young woman with green eyes. The detailed hologram steadies a clay vessel on her head with one hand. A snarling silver wolf approaches, fangs bared. The girl folds long legs beneath her sarong and sits, erect on her knees, at eye-level before the predator. The two lock eyes until the animal's growls turn to sobs, for the wolf has morphed into a shivering white-skinned child of indeterminate gender. She lifts the little face by the chin and their filthy yellow hair falls back to reveal parched lips. The child's mouth opens wider until, like a baby bird, its entire face is an open mouth. Standing, the girl pours water from her vessel over their face and hands and the mouth snaps shut. The two are grinning now, clean and radiant. The child stands to offer the heroine a dripping wet high-five. The magical girl returns the gesture and when their palms collide, iridescent water droplets crystalize mid-air. Then twinkle and scatter as they are now firefly-like winged insects.

And then, in the sparkling and winking appears Nicole, the host. Fradine's pulse quickens and the hologram meets Fradine's gaze. She mirrors Fradine's excitement with the same. Her mouth drops open as if taken by surprise. She covers her mouth with one hand as though she can hardly believe it. Fradine waves back, reflexively, and when Nicole offers her a glass of sparkling white wine she reaches out to accept it. But Nicole was only joking and she pulls back, laughing. Gives Fradine a wink as she takes a sip herself.

"Delicious! This is an absolutely delicious Riesling from the Western Cape of South Africa. In a few minutes we'll talk about new ways of pairing it. But first. But first! Can we discuss that intro? The music, the animation, the entire production was just. . . I mean, wow! I mean really, just wow! Simply amazing and apropos, I think, given what's been in the news all week. And can we just agree right now that piece of 4-D art – brought to you by our brilliant summer interns – is the very definition of wonder. Yes? Can we agree to that? Think, for just a sec, consider what we mean when we use that word. Wonder. Wonder!

"We love u Nicole!"

"You get the photo? They all here!"

Even Fradine, overcome with the holographic theater clapped twice to send a bouquet of rainbow hearts.

"My name is Nicole Thibidaux and this is Gracious Living. Welcome! Now, some of you are old friends so you know what comes next, but if you're new to the LiveCast I'll fill you in real quick. I like to start with a grounding meditation. Just a little something to set the tone for a peaceful yet productive day. Best part? It takes just fifty-eight seconds. That's less than one minute, folks! Let's get started. Close your eyes, please. Close your eyes with me and think of a time when you felt overwhelmed... just completely overwhelmed... with wonder."

11.

The Yellow Rope

Fradine plants a targeted advert on Nicole's computer in a successful bid to get inside. But what in god's hell is up with the demon-baby?

Available:

Clean Mother's helper babysitting,

Housework and Errands Gladly Completed.

Je parle français.

As Fradine stood heavily in the living room (wrapped up like a chocolate!) in her funny nylon dress — the sort of dress only an immigrant could find appropriate for a summer day in the Louisiana heat — Nicole pitied and loved her.

From the sunken living room sofa Ada squinted and smiled, encouraging. Leaned forward for a better look at the thick, sad thing. Squeezed and folded

into a cream-colored blazer. Ruffles poking out and
Ada counted not one but two diaphanous layers of
pink skirt (but exactly like the Saint Valentine's
Day chocolate!)

As the painful syntax and stilted carriage promised,
Fradine lacked both wit and charm. And yet. She
did seem respectful, honest and suitably cautious as
she fielded questions from mother and daughter.

Studying medicine, mesdames.

Enjoy the reading and the cooking activity.

No time for boyfriends, mesdames.

Fradine did speak lovely French (exquisite!) and
her manners were nice. Nice enough. A night
student at the university, she could come every
weekday morning, which would take the burden off
of Ada, although Ada insisted it was no burden at
all. And Nicole, a keen judge of character, decided
right then and there that beneath Fradine's coarse
exterior was a gentle soul. Ouais, this thick-
waisted, flat-eyed, picky-haired Haitian girl would
be a sturdy yet malleable addition. Giving her dense
flesh a squeeze, Nicole drew the girl out of the
foyer, down two little steps, and into the living
room proper. Front and center stood a Victorian
baby carriage, a navy-blue antique with a sweeping
hood.

When Fradine balked before the gaping mouth of the pram, Nicole pressed her manicure deeper into the girl's forearm. The pinch startled and the girl bent in, fixed her lips, but. Empty? Nothing there but a clump of wrinkled linen. Is this a house of crazy? Fradine must wonder if she should run. But then pop open a pair of small black eyes, and, well, there it was. A sallow little face halved by a white crocheted skull cap. A poached egg of a face, the rest bundled up in linens.

"Ohla-" Fradine began but was sliced by an unbaby-like howl.

Nicole swept her baby up. "Qu'est-que—? Wet again?" She laid the tiny body flat to her chest and shoulder. "Not wet," she said, eyebrows raised she glanced toward her mother. Ada responded with an exaggerated shrug. Nicole murmured into her infant's fat neck but Charlotte was already quieting. She took great gulps of air and hiccupped. With Fradine blocked from view, Charlotte came to peace. Nicole, frowning, peered into the wrinkled, unpurpling face. "So much terrible noise! So much fuss, and for what Angélique?"

Having exhausted herself, the infant slept and Ada cluck-clucked. "My golden grande-bébé, my sweet golden grand-bébé."

And yet. To white people, and also to Fradine, Nicole's baby appeared more jaundiced than golden. A cradle of urine, Fradine was thinking when Nicole passed to her the sleeping child. Fradine accepted and cradled the infant against her bosom with competence. Nasty yellow thing.

Nicole and Ada looked on, exchanged a glance, and just like that, C'est décidé. Little Miss Fussy was in good hands with capable, unassuming Fradine. This was meant to be! Certainly providence sent to them this lumpy black gem, this diamond in the rough. And who knows? Over time, and under the care of this Fradine, Charlotte might develop a thicker layer of skin (not too much thick, but. Ouais, d'accord.)

Such a fragile vessel, la p'tit miserable. Where Nicole was tight and dark, her child was broad and blending. Where Nicole was crisp and sharp, her child was blurred and yielding. And yet, poetry aside, Charlotte was a true miracle of modern obstetrics and every nurse in the unit made time to come see. The delivery was one for the books, for when the surgeon sliced open Nicole's belly there was Charlotte, neck and chest and limbs looped and wrapped in her mother's cord.

"Like some sort of cocoon," a young nurse would later recall.

"And a lot of lanugo! The dark Italian kind," the night supervisor would reply, not disagreeing. A chuckle. "Okay, I really shouldn't say this but you know that wild animal HelloCast? Live Nature?"

"Yeah no wait it's Lost Nature!"

"Yeah yeah. Lost Nature. It just popped in my head. That one did you see with the big-ass snake—"

"It's always a python or something. That show is so fake,"

"They rescue this baby mon—"

"What?!"

"This sweet little baby monkey . . .from this enormous Boa constrictor!"

"Holy shit I saw that! My brother made me watch! It was a Burnese Python and I totally remembe—"

Yelps of laughter from both women now. They bend together their heads, covering mouths with hands, eyes tearing, shoulders shaking. It was just after lunch.

In the days to follow Nicole would examine every inch of her baby. Underweight but not by much, Charlotte's veins glowed blue beneath her thin skin. Tracing the pattern of veins with the tip of one finger, the new mother would think of the dry membrane just beneath the shell of an Easter egg. Discomforted by that permeability; she had click-clack locked those thoughts away, quick.

Motherhood had made a fearless, modern woman out of Nicole, and Ada was sometimes impressed. These days she might even ask her daughter's opinion on shoes or bags: "Ces moderne, n'est-ce pas? Okay! Je bien compris, Nicole!"

C'est décidé. Fradine would learn the schedule. Each morning, a brisk walk in the pram. Past the shops and through the park. The flower-cart man, an old Dominican, would nod in silent appreciation, but the Chinese dry cleaner liked to flirt: "Big-eye lady! Big smile! Black and Beautiful Black Beauty!"

And Nicole, teeth shining, would flirt right back, "Alrighty now! You'd better settle down, now!" That's how they would talk. Nicole's laughing black eyes reflecting like a prism, a splash of hot oil on sizzling hot blacktop. The dry cleaner would hang his head in mock abashment.

"Perhaps I should speak with your wife," she might continue.

"No need! No need! I am so sorry! So so sorry!" he would beg, eyes stretched open

wide in simulated fear. And then they would laugh.

Charlotte's eyes were black too, but matte. They absorbed like sponge tissue. Charlotte would gaze up from the pram and drink and drink their laughter, how it slathered over all the things not be said. (note: exhausted. Turn her over on her stomach when the eyes bcm 2much)

Fradine had nothing to fear. Emergency phone numbers are right here written down and she must never hesitate to ask Ada Maman for any little thing, no matter how small. Nicole extended her arms and Fradine passed back to her the sleeping baby. Nicole transferred the child back into the depths of the pram.

Yes, yes, certainly Fradine would return Monday morning. She was grateful for the opportunity. Ouais, ouais, 7:30 sharp. Fradine is never late.

Later that evening mother and daughter ate tinned sardines with crackers and olives and finished the rest of the chardonnay. The two would speculate.

"Peut-etre . . .perhaps the girl Fradine is too black?" Ada suggested naughtily, a hand to her puffy cheek. Ada's still smooth skin was light-catching tan. Bright, like cheap kitchen furniture. The women shared a chuckle for that was ridiculous! A baby is innocent. Anyway, the Rousseau's are too sophisticated a family for that sort of idiocy. Provincial negro nonsense.

"It's not that, mom," This from Nicole, too quickly. "Lotte's accustomed to beauty. C'est naturel, n'est-ce pas? She simply doesn't like Ugly." And mother and daughter swallowed their giggles in guilty good humor again.

Beneath Nicole's tired old joke, however, was a pinpricking she could not name, nor upon which did she wish to dwell. The deepest brown of her two siblings, Nicole was jungle hardwood. She got it from her father. Ada was fair as pine tree pulp. When Nicole was a very little girl she had been desperate for a puffy sweater the color of cherry blossoms. For six weeks a yellow pony-tailed mannequin – a girl with a satchel – posed in the window of Dillard's. But shopping for school clothes Ada tried to distract. Over here, Nicole! Justlook at this twin set! ButNicole would not be distracted. From the top of the elevator she pleaded and begged until Ada, pumps biting her feet and weighed down with packages, reached out and snatched her eldest daughter by the arm. She jerked her in close: "You stop this foolishness Nicole you are too dark to wear pink!

Nevermind. Both Nicole and Ada had every reason for looking forward, not back. And both she and her mother slept well that night, and also the night after that. You cannot blame them! How could they possibly be expected to know why thick-legged Fradine was humorless and stiff.

The next day was Monday. Dressed crisp-crisp for work, Nicole gazed into Charlotte's face and pushed the pram three quarters of the way to the park, Fradine plodding behind.

"What will we see in the park today, I wonder!" Nicole sang. Charlotte's eyes were hardly big enough to drink in her mother's song.

"Will we see ducks? Will we see squirrels?"

Charlotte blinked her little wet eyes.

"Will you show them to big sister Fradine? Nous grande-soeur, Fradine? Belle Fradine?

Charlotte slept. Nicole beckoned Fradine forward, beckoned her with urgent flips of her slender hand tipped in pale polish. She slowed but didn't stop. Kept the carriage moving forward but pivoted to the side until both of Fradine's blue-black hands could grip the handles. Now it was Fradine pushing the carriage and Nicole clapped her hands with exaggerated delight. She squeezed Fradine's thick shoulders and fairly danced to the trolley headed east to downtown.

And Fradine pushed the pram for nearly an hour, into the park and around the giant slide and the seesaw and the princess garden and the Japanese maple. It was boiling hot, but under the trees, sheltered from the sun, a breeze dusted over her skin whenever the branches rustled. Like a powder puff, barely perceptible, a dry kiss. Fradine let her mind drift. What might she have for dinner? Last night's cell-shrimp was a delicious surprise! More like shrimp than actual shrimp . . .

A whimper from the pram.

"C'est bon, li bon, bebe," Fradine murmurs. But the mewling increases and Fradine must stop to investigate. Baby and nanny lock eyes and then . . .and then how she screamed! Charlotte howled and shrieked like a demon while passersby frowned their annoyance. Fradine paid them no mind because now, before her eyes! Mud flecked with blood, chunks of white bone mixed in with something like tar seeping into the inside of the formidable pram.

Then came a disembodied suggestion, breathed into both Fradine's ears: "Why not fish it out? Poor little fish!"

Less of a suggestion, perhaps, than the languid command of a woman unaccustomed to contradiction. "Why should a baby choke on fear," continued Mam'zelle Erzulie Freda, in her old-fashioned French. In her voice thick and gravelled from centuries of indulgences. A voice that absolutely was not Fradine's voice, although it issued from the lips of Fradine.

Now Fradine howled with Charlotte, a terrible duet

as bubbling, fomenting, viscous filth came licking up and over the antique linen, encircling and preparing to swallow the sallow little face.

Fradine plunged her hands into the muck and held the baby to the warmth of her breast.

"That's it, ma chou," purred Mam'zelle Freda, the mercurial lwa of luxury and sanctuary. "Apres tout," she continued, "who wants to eat a mud baby?"

If Fradine had any idea of what the lwa Erzulie Freda might have said, it most certainly was not that. Fradine startled and her hands shook. She nearly dropped Nicole's only child—head first—on the hot concrete. She pulled the infant tight to her chest, squeezing it there. And then Fradine saw herself from above, she was out of her body and looking down from a great height. It was shocking! And Mam'zelle Freda was gone.

Fradine quieted herself and peered into the bundle of wet linen. Charlotte was watching, absorbing, the face of her nanny Fradine. Fradine held her tight and then Charlotte gave a sigh and closed her eyes. She breathed in the scent of Fradine.

12.

Fradine Makes Clean

On the Floating French Quarter, a friendly Security and Surveillance Associate saves a mother-daughter team from embarrassment.

Being nearly 3:30 PM on a Sunday, Café Tous le Monde is stuffed with genial C8 patrons. Anchor tenant of the exclusive Floating French Quarter, Café Tous is generally a Low Actionables Risk assignment. Even so, one must stay alert and Safety and Security Inspector FradineT-36 has little trouble in this regard. Her tolerance for monotony falls within the acceptable range, according to the GenAssess. Not as high as the average American new hire, but her data processing and hand-eye reaction speed more than compensates.

Her program advisor liked to say, by way of introduction, "Here she is, Mam'zelle Fradine la formidable! You must watch out for that one. A computer for a brain, ouais, c'est vrais, ca!

Scores like hers could have landed Fradine any gig

in the University database, pretty much. But she likes AI and gadgets, and she prefers to work alone. Fradine is one of this year's Student Intelligence Scholars, a program directed by Haiti's National Security Program, so of course her scores are high. The hiring managers at The Cafe Corp had no way of knowing that, of course, so she just offered up her DNA. Like everyone else.

Fradine stifled a yawn. This is her second double this week. Pushing her luck? Possibly unwise if she is to lead study group. Something with the pediatric lympha— Headzup-Whodat! Headzup-Whodat! A series of whoops in her earbuds while her gloscreen flashes red to eyeball-piercing white. Not for long, though, as she has already swiped the SpeedRoller to RECEIVED. The whooping halts mid-whoop.

Meaty yet agile fingers skate over the SpeedRoller as T-36 guides a ladybug-shaped Pollinator over and around the questionable party of two. She swipes down and across; pulls up their summary data:

RLTNSHP: Directp-c-s. BC-group6⬦ reg #645, matern haplgrp #5654.

Two colored women, Louisiana indigenous. Mother is Ada Devereaux, 57. Daughter is Nicole, 23. T-36 swipes down for more data. Social Credit scores respectable enough. Some amount of political agitation on the fraternal side in a past generation, but nothing recent. T-36 zooms in on the pair of adult women, non-white, who hover near the door as though expecting to be seated. Old-fashioned types, she thinks. A bit overdressed.

Adjusting the audio, T-36 filters out the ambient noise until the Pollinator catches good sound. Now she can differentiate between the cupped vowels of what she quickly determines to be Creole French. Error message—the security software begs to differ. Nothing but a "Local Minority Dialect" of the North American Southeastern block. The pair would be offended, if they knew, and she might have been offended for them if it weren't for the fact that she'd grown accustomed to minor slights like that in the nearly four weeks she'd spent in the United States. Their crumpled French was certainly adequate, if not quite that of Pétion-Ville or Paris.

No cause for alarm, at any rate. No security threat. And this right here is possibly an example of a situation in which one might use a colloquialism. An idiome. Qu'est-qu'on dit? C'est ça un . . .the tempest in the teapot.

She says it aloud: "Tempest-in-the-teapot!" The sharp clicks followed by softer sounds make for tricky pronunciation (opportunity 4forshadowing okay solved these are the other idioms she has learned. DONE!) —throw baby with the bath water.   A   roosting   hen" HappyasaPiginapoke?American culture through folklore for foreign students Monkeyinthemiddle chickensbefore they hatchpotcallsthe kettlebell— black"

and she means to say it again. Is interrupted, however, by a series of warning beeps.

Standby for possible actionable intel. Standby, please.

Chin resting on her fist, T-36 waits for the Ladybug 102 Bioscanner to complete its rotations over and around the two females. An electric-white flash and then confirmation — the girl is nearly eight weeks pregnant. T-36, growing impatient, swipes up for more data. D'accord. The pregnancy, this rendezvous — something here may be of some small importance. The father? Not government. He may be important to some private entity, though. This last is simply deduction for it would explain the complete redaction of his personal details. Intriguing! And yet, still nothing. No more intel, nothing to do with Café security.

T-36 taps in the three-digit dismissal code.
Hesitates, then tags the pair with an orange Follow.
Who could fault her for an abundance of caution?
No harm, surely, in taking an interest.

Mother and daughter stand just inside the door,
distracted by the moving picture screen. The glass
wall brightens with full spectrum lighting. Coffee
beans, red and ripe, rustle in shaded beds of green.

Ada Devereaux is soft and yellow, with neat plump
calves under nylon stockings. Feet tipped in black
heels chink-chink on the tile and all around her is a
bustlingness.

The daughter is smaller-boned and browner-
skinned. Eyes are red-rimmed and moist, with
shoulders pulled up tight, closer to her ears than
is graceful. Mother's voice rings out stubbornly
cheerful. While her bottom lip trembles and her
own throat just squeaks. At any rate, it appears they
must find their own seats and mother, at least, is
unperturbed.

D'accord, Nicole! This is not . . . le grande chose.
We make do!

Finding the booths occupied, they consider a table.
Two of the bistro-style tables are free. A moment
of reflection before the two exchange glances.
Unsuitable! How would they look — legs perched
high in the air and behinds on display — slipping
off on the edges every-which-way.

Mother's eyes narrow. Perhaps the second to the
last booth is unoccupied. On closer inspection one
must so surmise. Recently abandoned – tabletop
littered with a half-eaten beignet on a snowdrift of
powdered sugar, a crumple of greasy napkins, an
empty ceramic cup.

"C'est bon, ça," murmurs the girl, preparing to slide
in.

"But there is no way of telling!" says the elder,
with an exaggerated shrug. A restraining hand on
her thin arm, she speaks to her daughter in rapid
French. Nicole must find the end of the line and
place their order. In the meantime, one of the
aproned boys will clear away the filth. Maman will
see to it.

The brown girl hesitates. The queue snakes around
glass cube table tops and then along the plate glass
wall. Nicole proceeds, with reluctance. She plucks

her way between tiny tables and chairs, one hand fluttering over her abdomen.

The yellow woman smiles after her daughter until the girl is blocked from view. She scans the crowd for a uniform. There he is, a young man in a loose fitting apron. Hovering — mantis-like — over the condiment rack, wiping and reordering napkins and sugars. Bright yellow hair curls over his forehead like a bathroom tissue cherub. He has the sort of upper lip that bends up at each corner. Forever smiling, even at rest. A sneering clown mouth!

The older woman's gaze is hard now, and T-36 jumps in her chair, startled by the high-pitched escalation warning. She taps onto her screen a short sequence and hits SEND 2. PGR 6.

The aproned boy swallows hard, a lump of cartilage tracking the gulp. A tapping on his wrist.

PSSBL(!)THRT. DRK㊛55+

He pivots, spins to his left. Nothing — wrong way. He spins back around, heart pounds, exhaling from his mouth. Facing her now.

Nicole's mother makes a wild gesture over the mess. "Someone sits here, no?"

"I suppose," he shrugs, breathing hard but feigning indifference.

"Is it yours?" she trills like a parrot, plump yellow hands fluttering over the mess.

"No ma'am!" bewildered, the boy lopes toward the kitchen, moisture spreading over his upper lip.

"C'est incroyable, ca!" she calls after him, hands in mid air. He stops, presses a button on his watch, comprehension flushing his cheeks.

"No ma'am, it's not mine. But I will clear it now," he says, recovered.

Stick insect legs carry him to the offending booth. Soiled napkins are tossed into the oversized cup. Saucer with donut chunk are next plucked from the tabletop. Balancing these on the fingertips of one hand, the boy, avoiding her glower, disappears into the kitchen.

The yellow lady maintains her standing position by the booth. Soon he will return to wipe away the sticky crumbs. She casts about for Nicole. The line doesn't seem to have shortened any. Two minutes pass. Three.

She is past impatient; the young man has vanished. Her face registers anger, first, then resolve. Turns her attention to the booth. From a shiny black handbag she produces a packet of facial tissues. Takes one out and then another. Scrubs the table's surface, rubbing furiously over the gummy places, over the damp rings left by cup and saucer. She sweeps the powdered sugar to the ground. She rubs in small, energetic circles.

Having punched in the dismissal code T-36 has back in her swivel chair, perspiring.

Nicole returns, bearing a tray with two oversized ceramic bowls of coffee, steam curling from their mouths. Ada sweeps the spent tissues to the ground. Eyes on her mother's face, Nicole wobbles the tray, lands it. caution.

"D'accord maman?"

"Maintenant, d'accord!" crows the mama. "Sit down, Nicole. Ça, c'est bon!"

SSI-36. Incident Report#001: Loc (LAT/LOG) DATE TimeStart :00TimeEnd :00 conclusion: EMPLOYEE OBJECT react. approp. medium average OK. StandDown order issued. Deescalation performance score 8.5. SUBJECT THREAT issued dated note. CopyFiled OK OK.

Fradine's NSEP letter

06/06/2040
Fradine Masseaux
696 Jacmel
(123) 4562345
DidiMasseaux@HelloCast.com

Chère Mlle. Masseaux:

I am pleased to award you a graduate scholarship for study under the auspices of the Haitian Security Training Education Program (HSTEP). Competition for scholarships in this sixth year of the program was especially intense. The merit panel and the standing committee of Old Black Ones selected you based upon your record of outstanding academic achievement as well as your demonstrated commitment in seeking to understand more deeply issues of international security.

As you know, the Program was created to ensure Haiti's future by the nurturing of a cadre of informed young adults able to operate in this new era marked by the decline of the imperial powers of the 20th century.

The Program will provide you with generous funding to be used to augment studies in your chosen field of computer science at the Xavier University Graduate School of Engineering in Baton Rouge, Louisiana. However, you will be expected to seek out a series of part-time employments, in various fields, to gain first-hand understanding of the application of programming theory to real-world situations.

In your case, M. Masseaux, the venue for your ethnographic field work will be within the militarized semi-autonomous Southeastern Block of the United States of America.

Although this is a particularly hazardous part of the post-industrial world, we trust that you have confidence in your government to do all we can to provide you with levels of comfort and security to which you are accustomed.

As one of only 200 scholarship recipients for 2040, you can be especially proud of your achievement. You have demonstrated motivation, academic rigor, and a commitment to your field of study.

We send you abroad with the blessings of our ancestors as you strive to gain the knowledge and insight necessary to contribute to international understanding cooperation, peace, and justice on our shared planet. And more of the same to your home country, the Republic of Haiti.

It is you, chère Fradine Masseaux, of whom our ancestors dreamt.

Sincerely yours,

Claudine Gruyère
Claudine Gruyère
Director of University Development

Department of International Peace and Justice
National Defense Université de'Haïiti
"Observation, Inquiry, Action"
Port-au-Prince 12345678

About the Author

Aina Hunter has been seeding disinformation and propaganda since fourth grade. She learned to turn coping mechanisms into a skill set which led, indirectly, to a career in public journalism at some of the most fearless alt.weekly news papers in the world where she reported on agriculture, farmed animals, sexual abuse, female bodies. Today she is a grower of mugwort and a boiler of seitan. She lives with her wife in a haunted stone house in western Massachusetts.

About the Publisher

Whisk(e)y Tit is committed to restoring degradation and degeneracy to the literary arts. We work with authors who are unwilling to sacrifice intellectual rigor, unrelenting playfulness, and visual beauty in our literary pursuits, often leading to texts that would otherwise be abandoned in today's largely homogenized literary landscape. In a world governed by idiocy, our commitment to these principles is an act of civil service and civil disobedience alike.

Made in the USA
Middletown, DE
26 September 2021